THE LEGEND OF JACK HOLLOW

William Strickler

Dedication

This book is dedicated to my mother and father. They were always there with love and support for all of their family and friends.

Acknowledgment

I would like to express my gratitude and special thanks to all the old gunfighters of the Wild West—may their souls rest in peace. Without them and their recorded chronicles, the inspiration for such an adventurous tale may not have been entertained. Also, a special thanks to Book Writing Cube for editing and publishing this book.

Table of Contents

About the Author

William Strickler lives in Lincoln, CA. He lives on a farm and has a beautiful wife, children, and grandchildren. Many animals live on the farm, too, wherein there is a corn maze that, in the month of October, is believed to be haunted by the ghost of "Hungry" Jack Hollow...

Page Blank Intentionally

Chapter 1
Hungry Jack Hollow

Back in the days of the gunfighters, many years ago, during the gold rush era of the mid-1800s, in the newly founded state of California, there was a bustling mining town that its inhabitants called Lincoln. It was an often traveled stagecoach stop and railroad depot. The train station was located at the western end of town, and its rails extended northwest and south. It bellowed with the sounds of the day's visiting locomotives, followed by its whistle and the squeal of its brakes. The hiss of its steam engine was comforting to some, and the whole town would feel its rumbling vibration when it pulled into the station.

This particular railroad stop was where ninety percent of all the raw gold that miners prospected ended up. It was usually exchanged for paper money, twenty-dollar gold pieces, and silver coins. There, crates of raw, unrefined gold were stockpiled in vaults and then boarded onto trains after being loaded into wooden boxes clad with iron chains and locks.

It always left the town well-protected by many armed guards, army rangers, railroad men, and Pinkerton agents. Its destination was a mystery on a monthly schedule that only the town banker and the lead conductor were supposed to

1

know. It always left town a secret, but the question was always how well-kept that secret was. The town itself had many secrets of its own. There were many chilling tales of robbery, murder, buried treasures, and even cannibalism.

Jack H. Hollow was born in the very busy town of Lincoln, California, in the year 1852. Two years after California joined the union. It was a time when guns and gold ruled the land. The 'H' stood for Huber, but his nickname as an infant was 'Hungry,' called so for his insatiable appetite. He lost his innocence at a young age; Hungry had grown up in the back alleyways of the gambling saloons, under the porches and the walking boards of the boardwalks, and would hide out beneath the floors of the back powder rooms of the whore houses. He had found a tunnel that went under some of the rooms and would spend time carving out new passageways and playing in the dirt. Sometimes, the madam would sneak him into the card room to save him from freezing to death in the chill of the winter months. The smell of fresh burning tobacco and warm air was like a hug to him. A small, slender boy mumbling, "I am born of worms, I am born of worms, I am born of worms…"

Jack was always hungry, even when he had eaten well. He was the only boy in town who was not cared for by loving parents. He was basically an orphan who spent a lot of his time hidden in dark places; he would hide under stairwells and play under the back porches of the whore house in the dirt. Spiders, worms, and flies had kept him close at all times—often, he would watch the maggots crawling out of dead rats and see them transitioning from larvae to winged flying bugs that would swarm him as he hid under the stairways and boardwalks.

He collected coins that fell through the cracks between the boards. As he grew up, he studied books and was self-taught, learning to read from wanted ads and discarded newsprints. A prostitute had shown him how letters were written and how they were pronounced. Jack's mind, like his features, was sharp; he studied the gunfighters and spied on drunk gamblers as they passed along the walking boards. He also watched the gold exchange and all the miners coming into town, most of them traveling on horseback or stage coaches fresh off the Washington trail.

He also kept a watch on the railroad station's activities. There were a lot of shootouts there. He would run out and collect whatever he wanted off the dead and always had a stash of knives and bullets, belts, guns, coins, gold, boots, and hats. He collected all kinds of stuff from a young age and hid his loot in different areas all over the town.

He also liked to look up the dresses of the dancing girls and prostitutes and see their colorful leg stockings, garter belts, and flashy satin lace undergarments. He was born as the only son of a gunfighting gambler and an opium-addicted, fiery, red-headed prostitute.

Hungry witnessed many brutal killings at a young age and also many other things that a young soul should never have endured. He had straight, reddish-brown hair, green eyes that pierced into your soul, wicked thin lips, and high, pointy cheekbones. Even as a young boy, he looked like an evil, red-headed leprechaun. By the time he was nine, he had killed his first human. Soon after that, he lost the upper half of his lip and left face cheek to a wild alley dog that attacked him. He had beaten the dog several times before for stealing his food.

The town medicine man said that he was a restless and hungry spirit and he would find his way one day. He gave Hungry a lot of food. He was the only man Hungry would listen to as a young boy. He showed Hungry how to hold a knife, use a bow and arrow, and swiftly draw out his pistols. Looking at that boy and his jagged, rotten teeth, missing half his face and lips, was scary as hell.

Hungry would draw his two guns and rapid fire. He killed every dog he came across after that and ate most of them, preserving their hides and ears. He even ate their puppies a couple of times. He soon moved on to killing men, mean drunks, shifty card cheaters, perverts, and women abusers.

He had many ways of ending their days. He would pour

a mixture of lighter fluid and kerosene from a whiskey flask on them, strike a match, and toss it at them, watching the spreading short flames changing colors from blue to green to the longer yellow and orange ones and then to a full red blaze, with them screaming in agony. Their bodies would be shaking and twitching violently as they shrieked and squealed. He learned from his first victim not to get too close.

He only picked the men he felt were really deserving of it: the super cruel, mean ones. One of the men who had beaten his mother got what he had coming. Jack lit him on fire and slashed him several times with an Indian-made obsidian knife. First, he speared him through the leg with an arrow he had found from under the stairs. Then he came out from under the stairs and stabbed him in the belly with a pitchfork, and as he crouched, Hungry cut him into pieces, running in circles around him while singing Sunday church hymns that he would listen to from under the walking boards. This particular drunk had really hurt his mother. Hungry stole his hat, boots, silver dollars, gold, and guns and lit him on fire with a coal oil and kerosene mixture that he had in his flask.

He bought his first bottle of whiskey and ate buffalo leg steaks at the saloon that night. He liked the way folks watched him with his new, slightly oversized boots and hat. "Whiskey sour, bitches!" he would yell at the prostitutes and bartenders. Donned in the cowboy apparel, gunnery, and gold from his first kill. He fancied himself a gunman now as he strolled along the walking boards.

Chapter 2

Almost A Teenager

He was almost a teenager. His father was hardly ever around—he could only recall him being there a couple of times earlier in his childhood, and they were never pleasant memories. His father was always on the run as an outlaw and was an abuser of women. He was usually driving stolen cattle along the Santa Fe trail, hundreds of miles away, stealing cattle, murdering the meek and robbing townspeople and gamblers, killing any decent man along the way.

Jack's father was born into very bad circumstances in the time of the economic depression of the 1820s. He was the only son and survivor after an Indian raid and massacre. Hungry's father had watched his parents being pierced with arrows, skinned and scalped, and had lived through it. He had been partially scalped himself and was shot in the belly with an arrow before he got away. After that, he swore vengeance against every Indian and white man. Hungry's father blamed the trail boss for leading them into a trap and took his wrath out on any man in a position of leadership. Not soon after that, he turned completely homicidal, killing and even eating parts of the women, men, lawmen, and bandits that crossed his path.

Hungry's father was also known to ride with the Barter

gang. He had met Richard Barter, also known as Rattlesnake Dick, when he first came to California to stake a claim at gold mining in Folsom. Unfortunately, the gold mine claims were all taken up, so he resorted to horse thievery and gold robbing. Hungry got word that his father, also known as Snake, was with the Barter gang when they robbed the shipments of gold, being led by a mule team and wagon sent down the Trinity mountains from the Eureka and Klamath river mines.

The mule train was stopped just outside of Nevada City, where part of the barter gang heisted $80,000 in gold bullion. The load became too heavy for the wagon and mules, so they divided it and hid half of the gold along the trail. Most of the gang died in a shootout with the Wells Fargo posse coming down the hill, and it is said that half of their loot still remains hidden in the Trinity mountains today.

Hungry had never heard from his father. After that news, he wondered if he died in the shootout and was buried out on the plains somewhere in an unmarked grave. He wondered if he got away or if he was just shot up and left to bleed out someplace for the coyotes and buzzards to pick his carcass. Jack didn't give him much thought after that, though—he was getting hungry.

Some of the traits that his father had were passed on to him: a son who was twice as mean and violent. Hungry lived through many horrible events before he started wandering the trails alone. He had a burning hunger that could never be satisfied. He could eat five or six rabbits or even half of a large deer in one sitting. It was said he had several tapeworms from living off of the garbage in the back of the saloons. He was as slender as a twig. His long arms, neck, and legs gave him the look of a long predator insect.

Being on the open trail gave him a mild sense of comfort. He would feel it as the wind would rustle the leaves in the trees, and its breeze would blow the smell of the valley's wildflowers and long grass. In his later teenage years, he would wander along the mountain and valley trails until he spotted signs of humans. He would follow their tracks to find them, count their numbers, and number the targets. After quietly analyzing them, he would back off and lay low for a couple of hours and formulate his plan.

He was on the trail one day in his late teens when he realized he could smell the familiar scent of a type of meat he had been fed as a child. He came across the smell before he saw the burnt wreckage and charred remains of a lone stagecoach driver who had been torched to death. Only his smoldering burnt carcass and the blazing stagecoach remained. Indians must've set it on fire after stealing his horses as he was pierced with arrows that were barely rods of ash.

The smell tantalized his nostrils for days until he realized that his skank of a father had actually fed him human meat—he was sickened to know that he had eaten it and liked it, not knowing what it was. It had tasted like pork belly, he thought as he wandered along in the lone darkness, waiting for his new victims to lay down and rest for the night.

He listened to them argue for hours about how they should've never been on this trail, how they should've never left the comfort of their Santa Fe hotel, and how they should've never left their kid's dog Kipper with their mother and father to get eaten by the wolfs.

These were the times that pioneers were settling across the plains, or drifters were gathering supplies to mine for gold here and there. You could tell when they found gold— they would head straight for the big cities to drink and gamble and be at the doors of prostitutes. Along those trails, sharp, twisting canyons entwined by rocks and massive trees were where Hungry Jack Hollow had made his name. *"Beware of the jagged tooth, half-faced man who would steal your gold, bind you in leather straps, and eat pieces of you!"*

Much of it was exaggerated talk, whisperings in saloons, or ramblings of Westward-bound carpet baggers. Every saloon town was filled with its share of criminals. They were the prey who didn't have a prayer in church against Hungry. He noticed they were bedding down for the night—it was time to get a move on or light a shuck, as the old-timers would say, in reference to the times when corn shucks were used as candles and were lit to illuminate a pathway at night.

The moon was shining super big and bright this Halloween night, and it was Jack's 19th birthday. He was born on Halloween night and was left with the barmaids and call girls for most of his childhood life while his mother would run off with her elixirs and "John's" at the time. These were usually men who had struck good fortune, but their fortune and affinity for Jack's mother would only ever last a short while. She would come crawling back with more scars than the time before that, looking ten years older each time.

He first came upon the maid, who was still rambling something in her sleep about their dog Kipper. He slowly ran her over with the wagon cartwheel. She gasped for air, but by then, he had already broken her neck and shot the man she was with in the head and neck. He removed his boots, took the man's shoes, and threw them both in the fire. Usually, he burned everything before he would leave, but this time, he only burned their shoes. It was one of his quickest and cleanest kills as he was still thinking about his childhood in his head and how his mother always left him to the other whores of whatever town she was in at the time.

Jack had spent the first portion of his infant life growing

up in the upstairs rooms of the Silver Dollar saloon in Marysville. It was the most comfortable time of his life. His first words were "bitch" and "piece of shit," spoken before the age of one. He was well-fed there as there were many nursing mothers. His own mother had worked there for a few years before being exiled by the owner and all of the other girls. They could not condone her behavior nor trust her. They had offered to keep Hungry, but she refused and took him to Lincoln just to leave him with the call girls in that town.

There, as he grew, he would ponder the hymns and poetry readings from under the stage station platform. It was where he wrote his first poem:

Through the fields of green and streets of red
I steal the gold from all the dead
The sun, it shines on in chilled decay,
all in song and clouds of grey…
Where goes the pale ghost rider?
No one knows where he'd be…
Calm as dawn comes a man upon horseback
Is it the end of me?

He learned to make rhymes killing cold time to keep the winter freeze from taking him. He would mumble over and over while he nearly froze beneath the walking boards…

I am born of worms; I am born of worms

I am born of worms; I am born of warm
I am born of worms;
I am born of worms; I am born a worm; I am born of
warm…

He had never had any human friends around his age. He made friends with the flies and bugs that followed him around, and he had many of them all the time; they were all the friends he needed. Standing alone in the darkness of the shadows, he would gaze into the flames of the kerosene street lamps as some of the bugs would crawl out of his ears into his nose, through the holes of his face, around his rotten, jagged teeth, and back out of his nostrils. He wouldn't even blink an eye. A dank, musty earth smell rose from him; if you got too close, your eyes burned. In his younger days, he would usually be dirty and would always have some type of bug, lizard, or frog in his pockets.

Hungry decided it was time to round up all his gold and loot and look for a tall rock outcropping with memorable characteristics or a tall pine tree next to a creek somewhere. Those were some of his favorite spots to bury stuff. Jack's thoughts were his only companions as he traveled over the narrow rocky trails and pathways, traversing the trail through steep ledges that dropped to rock-lined riverbeds far below. He was headed south. *Was this world just a card game of carnage and death? Always dealing out the cards, never-ending, demanding everything you have, and bringing death and despair to its chosen victims.*

Hungry would watch all the different types of plants and animals on the Prairie as they would perish. Their carcasses would dry up or be eaten, and all would disappear, sometimes leaving gleaming bones to disintegrate. Tree limbs, once lush and endless green, were now stressed, dried up, and cracked into shades of gray and black. Hillsides eroded into arroyos that, like miniature desert plains, turned to sand.

At other times, while lying awake at night, alone on the trail under the vast canopy of starlight, he would think of how almost all living creatures are born to feed upon one another in an endless circle of frenzied feeding and feasting. He was just a morsel of salt and water; he, too, would soon be ingested and consumed by the next in line for food. Jack knew that he had to keep on striving forward in life at all times. The balance of nature was achieved by continual feeding.

Jack had an inner force of energy. It helped him stay alive through impossible odds as an infant and child. It took a lot of fighting and determination to survive—to not be eaten.

On this particular day, he was looking for a new cavern to hide some of his loot. This time, he had struck fortune by robbing some wanted outlaws who had just raided the local town's bank and had, unfortunately for them, met Hungry on their way out of town.

As he rode slightly off the pathway commonly used, he came upon an older gentleman. He was carving words into the side of an empty wooden Wells Fargo box. Hungry holstered his gun and said, "I mean you no harm, mister." He approached the man slowly, and they stared at one another for quite a while before Hungry spoke again, "You, sir, are Charlie Boyles, the famous stagecoach bandit." The gentleman looked at Hungry, his slender, sharp features dressed in the finest of cowboy boots, hat, and leathers.

The man replied, "Yes, among many things, my young friend. Some folks call me Black Bart, the gentleman bandit. It looks like you are in the trade yourself." He nodded towards Hungry's horse. Hungry had many rifles and four giant bags of gold strapped to his horse and saddle. There was no way to hide it. Usually, he would just kill anyone he came across. He did not deem Charlie a threat.

Suddenly, from the corner of his eye, he saw the ground cover move near the man. Instinctively, Hungry dove towards the movement, pushing his hands through the vines and leaves, grabbing the snake behind its head. Hungry then twisted it off. Charles immediately turned to him with guns drawn, completely oblivious to the rattlesnake that almost struck him. Hungry's movement was fast as lightning; he had never seen the likes of it before. The headless snake slithered and coiled itself around Hungry's arm as he stomped the head into the dirt. Hungry had seen people die from a rattlesnake's bite before. He'd seen a couple of face bites where the victim's flesh would swell up so much that it exploded.

He spent the afternoon with Charlie. They made coffee and roasted the rattlesnake on a stick on a small campfire. They ate it with biscuits that Hungry had kept in his saddle bag, wrapped in a square cut wrapping of burlap. Bart was the most sophisticated and stylish bandit of the time. Hungry had always admired him; he recited some of his poetry to Charlie. Jack was always intrigued by the words that went fluently together or phrases that would rhyme.

Knowing their fire would draw unwanted attention, they gathered their belongings for departure. Within minutes, they heard the sound of approaching horses. The riders were on the trail below. Hungry and Bart were watching from behind a manzanita bush on a rocky ledge outcropping. The trail narrowed before and after the outcropping, with a sheer-faced cliff on one side. Hungry led his horse away down the trail and tucked him behind a giant boulder. He saw Charlie's horse there as he grabbed three rifles and ran back.

With his lightning-fast speed, he climbed to the top of the giant boulder just as the posse was approaching. As soon as the lead man saw the two bandits, gunfire erupted. Hungry brought his lever action .40 caliber Winchester and had blasted holes in the heads of every one of them before you could blink. None of their pistols could even clear leather. The bodies were slouching forward on their mounts, revealing bleeding holes in the back of their heads the size of silver dollars. Their horses collided, and a few of them slid off the trail, toppling over the cliffside to the rocks and river in the valley below. The smell of the black powder from the gunfire was in the air, and one could hear the muffled screams from the men and the bellowing from the horses as they slid their hard rock landing. The other riders lay on the ground, bleeding as their horses scrambled back the way they came.

Black Bart looked at the kid in astonishment and awe and said, "Don't reckon I've ever seen anyone quite as fast with the rifle; I imagine you're a pretty good shot with those six irons as well." He was breathing fast and sweating. Hungry was reluctant to part ways, but he knew he had to cut a trail. He said, "It's been a pleasure, Mister. The sundown is coming fast, and we got places to get to, and I have gold to bury." Hungry flashed his half-faced wicked grimace, showing his scars and jagged teeth, but this time his smile was genuine. He headed back toward the trail they came from, ready to confront any horsemen that might appear. He wanted to make sure that Charlie Boyle would get away.

Hungry continued on his robbery spree, killing many lawmen and bandits. Days turned into months that turned into years that seemed to sweep by faster each time. He had acquired so much gold and other treasures that he was running out of places to hide it all.

One cloud-covered day under a canopy of silver, black, and gray, while traveling through an evergreen meadow walking beside his newest, favorite horse, he started thinking about companionship. Would he ever want or find anyone human, preferably female, compatible enough to accompany him? Who would have similar characteristics? He had never been interested in any person 'he had ever met—some of the hookers had pretty fiery souls, brutal face scars, and lunatic personalities, but he was not sure if he wanted to get too involved with anyone he knew would try to play him like a fiddle and steal his gold.

He dragged canvases with gold and jewelry along the crooked thorn brush-covered trail. Hungry came upon another pony express stagecoach and ambushed it, killing all its riders and passengers in a volley of rapid and accurate gunfire. It was full of loot. He emptied the coach, lit it on fire, and watched the burning flames change their colors from blue to green, yellow, orange, and red. The burning embers flew sideways in the wind as the dawn closed in around the twisted campfire. He wrote another poem that night when the moon was just a sliver.

The Legend Of Jack Hollow

Valleys that sprawl into oceans of canyon walls, lit by
burning, robbed stages…

Remanence of souls whispers of faces

All burning into ash, to leave there no trace of…

He came back to the present with a two-inch wooden
thorn stuck into his knee. He cursed and pulled it out; the
pain made him break into a sweat. Not long after, he started
getting a little cold and thought to himself, *"I best get out of
this part of the country within the next couple of days."* The
wind started to feel the chill of the winter months ahead. He
made his way from mining cabin to hunter's lodges,
slaughtering bandits and killing other lawmen and outlaws,
robbing banks, coaches, and trains along the way, making
himself home in their shelters for a day or two, using up their
supplies, and moving on.

Chapter 3

White Dove

The highlight of his trail wandering was stumbling across a ghost-skinned Indian girl with white feathers entwined in her hair. He met her at a watering hole near a giant mossy rock and an old broken-down sycamore tree. She had five eagle feathers and bleached white leather. She moved like the wind, elegant as sin. She was like satin, a princess to his prince of the mysterious macabre. He was afraid to talk to her. It was the only time he ever felt fear of anything. Even when the wild dog was chewing at his upper lip, he was still not scared, just pissed and wicked, evil and mean. She turned to him and glanced a smile just as arrows flew at her, piercing through her lower arm—one nearly caught her in the neck. She moved away with cat-like quickness and returned arrow-fire of her own. Hungry quickly attacked her bushwhackers, shooting each of them in both of their savage eyes with his new Colt single action .45s. Almost simultaneously, flying burning arrows pierced their necks. Their bodies twitched as they slid down the rocks from their hidden positions. They were on fire and were leaving a bright red blood trail leaking from their blown-out eyeballs.

He was a damn gifted shot with a good side iron, and he only kept the best equipment. But she surprised the hell out of him with burning arrows that fast. After watching their smoldering bodies quit twitching and convulsing, he looked over to see his newfound beauty between a rock and a giant log. She looked at him with the most beautiful eyes, one brown and one blue. She shot flaming arrows from her bow, which she could light in an instant with her flinted perfume bottle. She was the most beautiful thing he'd ever seen in his life. He realized at that moment that this was the first time in twenty-some years that he had felt sensual attraction for someone.

She glanced at him and made the suggestion for tobacco, indicating she wanted him to steal the tobacco from the dead ambushers. He quickly checked for more of them before gathering some of their belongings. He rolled and lit her a smoke. The attackers were two Indians. Were they from another tribe or some renegades on the scourge for anything they came upon? Where did she come from? Maybe she didn't have a tribe of her own, and she was a wanderer too—another lost soul walking on the lonesome trail, like a ghost traversing through the canyons, valleys, and towns, alone in their harsh, cruel world, raining death on everything that could be a threat to their existence.

He rolled her some more cigarettes, gave her some water from his canteen, and they stared at each other for a long while. They lit a campfire at night. The long fingers of flames grew crimson red and bright orange, flickering and reflecting off the jagged rocks towering over the water and trail. They roasted a couple of rabbits that Hungry had shot while searching for more attackers. He ate most of the meat. White Dove was amused by his appetite. The two of them moved closer together as an owl hooted in the night.

This night was different from any night he'd known. It was warm, and he was not alone. Purple hues with orange and red swathes of color filled the sky. As the fire dimmed, Hungry stared into her eyes for an eternity. He came back to his senses, realizing there could be more bushwhackers, so he quickly ran to higher ground and scouted the terrain again. After he was satisfied that they were alone, he made his way back to the little brook along the rocky-edged shoreline. He found her smoking her tobacco and waiting for him with devious-looking smiling eyes, one blue, another brown, set apart beautifully, with the look of a predator and killer. Pretty black eyelashes, as long as the legs of a spider curled away from them, but every other part of her body was draped in white.

"Do you remember ever seeing a white bird?" he thought to himself. Then, he recalled by the oceanside, they would swoop down on him as he walked the shoreline. The first time he had seen the ocean, he almost felt love for it, but it was always cold. After they shared a cigarette, Hungry made hand gestures as he spoke to her, slowly relating that she should stay in a little cave that he knew about, down the trail from them until morning, and then be on her way or stay wherever she wished. She wanted to follow, but he had to get away from her to think out a plan clearly.

He decided he would look after her for a while. He would look for a place where she would be safe—a secluded mountain trapper cabin or a stone cave for her to stay in. When they cross paths again, he would have food and tobacco he saved for her and shelter to offer. He would never harm her the way he did everything else—he usually left behind a carnage of death. The buzzards and coyotes loved him for all the carcasses he left along his trails. This time, he was, again, leaving behind dead bodies, but he was also leaving something that made him feel warm and… alive. He was on a different wave of satisfaction than he had ever felt with any human or madam.

He had not made many friends. The Indian shaman was his closest, and some of the gunfighting cowboys of the town had sort of became his allies. When he was 14 years of age, he did have an acquaintance with one of the last known living giants of the Sierra Nevada mountain range. He was a huge man, about 19 feet tall, and he lived in an enormous mountain cave. Hungry had met him hunting one day when he had killed more deer than he could carry. He remembered listening to stories in the saloons and gambling halls of the giant human-shaped creatures that would come to town, rip off the heads of the people, collect them in their huge animal pelt loin pouches, and eat their bloody twitching bodies. They would flip over the wagons with one arm and throw saddled horses through the windows of saloons and motels. They wore large animal bones and necklaces of human skulls, and they wrapped their faces in animal skins. Their hide was so thick that bullets would bounce off their skin. It was said you could shoot them through the eye, and that was the only way to kill them. The giant was hunting Hungry when he yelled at it, "I have no fear of you! My lead bullets will surely blind your eyes. How will you forage for food then, huge fellow?" He then shared his food with the giant, and they had become somewhat friendly. However, Hungry figured the giant would eat him in an instant if he let his guard down. He had a heap of bones at the mouth of his cave, which was full of human skeletons. Hungry still visited the giant once or twice a year, always with fresh meat of some kind, horses, lawmen, even some bandits. He would bring some of them still alive to watch him feast… until one day, the giant was just gone—all signs of him were erased, and his cave was empty.

Hungry was also always on the move. He had to stay busy; he was always pirating and hiding gold. He had a few of the local sheriff possies always looking for him, but they were freakishly always overmatched. They were so loud and clumsy and knew nothing about creeping into the darkness and being quiet. They never lasted more than half a week or two, but they always had good guns and gold.

He also liked tobacco, whiskey, and jewels. He would just bag them up by the burlap sack loads and take them to his local caves, all of the old mining tunnels down the Virginia town road.

Prospectors were moving north at the time, seeking bigger gold deposits, veins of gold in rocks of quarts instead of the tumbled pebbles and smashed pieces in rounded rocks found in the local American rivers and streams of Auburn ravine and Dodie's canal.

Several of his tunnels would cave in, but little did he care. As long as no one else had found his treasure, he could dig his way back in, usually. He thought about his White Dove. He would continue his search down the steep mountain canyon and up the other side to a cabin that he had remembered a few winters past. Was it still standing? Did it just have rats and mice? If so, they were good for eating if there was nothing bigger in the animal kingdom.

It was there after a few scrapes and bruises from climbing and crawling over huge rocks. The cabin stood almost hidden under broken trees, surrounded by an enormous eagle's nest of mountains with sharp, jagged boulders of granite and quartz. The trail to it was only accessible through a huge crack in a giant stone from the valley below. It was like a picture window to a hidden fortress in the mountain of rocks. The cabin still had a roof on it, but it was in need of repair.

He stayed the night there, eating a few rabbits and raccoons he had found who had tried to dig under the rocks. He lay on the porch overhang, found some old animal skins to wrap around him, and lit no fires but stayed there on the rooftop throughout the night, listening for any sounds of humans. It was almost completely silent that night; only the wind, coyotes, and a few crickets stirred. A brilliant falling star lit up the night skyline, illuminating the mountains' jagged rocks and a silhouette of the valley below.

Jack pondered about his white maiden. He wondered if she were thinking of him and still alive, if she were a Maidu or Iroquois. Was she Apache crossed with a Comanche? Part troglodyte? Albino? She had small bones in her neck that whispered air when she talked, and he faintly recognized her native language.

He would also think about the times his dad would put him in the wooden box, and all his friends would kick at it and stab knives into it. Some of them were freaks with bones in their faces. They said they were teaching him how to be meaner. They would drink and laugh, and it made him mean and a lot more cold and calculative. He would wait for them to stick a knife in the box and pull it through by the blade, cutting his fingers and hands just to wait for them to peer into its hole to see how he was doing. Jack would strike, piercing out their eye and calling them "bitches." He had pierced out several eyes during his time, but the dumbasses never seemed to learn.

Now that he had found his hunting cabin, he would spend several months preparing it while all the time checking in on his white maiden to make sure she had food and tobacco. Hungry had found a bigger cave higher on a rocky cliff where they had to use a thick rope with knots in it to climb up for entry, and then once they climbed inside, they would pull it back up. They had brought several rounds of ammunition up to the cave. Crates, an old Sharp 50s, an Octagonal Winchesters 40 caliber. Patterson 58. calibers and Whitworth .45s, with plenty of bullets. Hungry taught White Dove how to load and shoot every pistol and rifle he had. They were not fair game for any kind of intruders or an ambush; she did know how to shoot.

Jack had spent many long hours shooting off crates of ammunition with his guns. He would shoot until the gun barrels wore out or almost melted. After hijacking more guns, tobacco, whiskey, gold, and crates of ammunition from a traveling salesman, one day, he brought her home.

Chapter 4

The Hunter's Cabin

Her brown eyes shined like a polished raw diamond when she looked at the front door. A tear streamed down her cheek, and she looked at Hungry, smiling through her good eye.

She had suffered some ill fate, too, along the trail while sleeping on a rock outcropping. She had lost an arrow one morning while shooting at a quail, and she was looking for it when she found a mushroom she recognized as spiritual. She collected it and bit off a portion as she searched for the missing arrow. After hours of seeing super vivid colors and watching trees and rocks melt away, she laid down to rest and fell asleep. She had then become a victim of a buzzard attack. One bird had ripped off part of her eyelid and pierced a white scar into her blue eyeball. She could still see a blurred pattern through it; it seemed to be healing as she stared up at Hungry in admiration.

He opened the door for her. They spent the night inside the cabin. Bottled sparks illuminated the inside of its walls; Hungry had made them from an electric generator and piano wires he had salvaged from an old inventor. The inventor had some really sophisticated electronics for the 1800s. He was a true genius who created electrical devices that were motion-propelled, sun-powered, or driven by gears or wheels to create electricity.

Hungry had incorporated this into the hunting cabin, illuminating several rooms with the piano wires spiraled in mason jars. They were attached to bigger wires that led back to a generator that was turned by a hand crank or a paddle wheel mounted next to a little stream. They spent several hours cleaning out the cabin and ate more jerked meat before they went hunting and exploring past the meadow that lay beneath the canyons' towering sharp rock walls.

The night sky was radiant, glowing red and orange. Fires were burning all over the state and in the town of Sacramento. Wildfires had swept through and burnt a lot of the farms and local businesses. That night, Hungry and White Dove went on a vengeance-killing spree. The moon was full, and they had been together for almost one full year. He remembered the first time he had seen her shoot flaming arrows. Since then, they had been on a trail of mystery and adventure and a little killing. In many ways, they were of the same, born and orphaned, yet strong of spirit and soul.

They came upon a band of looters who had just loaded their wagons from the local town's jewelry stores and ammunition and gun depots. Hungry counted his targets— there were three wagons and 14 horsemen. They were coming down the trail as Hungry and White Dove were waiting, sitting on top of a high rock cropping, smoking tobacco, and oiling their guns. They first heard the sound of horses galloping—iron horseshoes clanging on rocks and earth rumbling. There was just enough light in the day to see the dust cloud of their caravan as it approached them.

This band of outlaw looters killed anyone in their path. They were a dirty band of drifters and looters. Stinky and unshaven, their clothes soiled and wrinkled brown and clay-colored from the dirt in which they laid. They approached closer, carriages and horsemen, dragging the corpses of a mutilated banker and the town sheriff's body behind them, dangling from the ropes of hangman's nooses. Hungry knew they would try to rob him for pleasure. He was standing on top of the rock as they approached. The lead rider saw him and brought the caravan to a halt. They had a few coaches filled with stolen goods. Hungry fired a couple of shots in the air from his six-shooter revolvers and then dove for cover behind the giant boulder just as their volley of gun fire erupted. They rode closer to the rock Hungry was hiding behind, shooting at him and yelling and hollering. Hungry returned a couple of shots, then quickly ducked for cover again.

Just then, he heard the thunder of his .44 caliber octagon barrel Winchester. White Dove had found a higher ground position on the backside of their trail and was blasting the soiled horsemen one at a time. The horsemen flew sideways from their mounts, slamming to the ground like rusty tin soldiers sitting atop metal horses blown over by a wild wind.

Hungry came out from behind the rock, running towards them with his pistols in each hand, rapidly firing his pearl-handled colt revolvers, killing the rest of their group and filling their carriages with gunfire. The horses were still at first, and then most of them ran back down the trail where they came from as their riders lay dead, sprawled on the ground, bleeding from their faces and necks into the dirt. Hungry watched as the half-remaining mutilated carcasses, which had already been dragged miles, were once again on the move, being pulled by riderless horses back to the town they came from. They were bumping, twisting, and skidding along, hardly leaving a blood trail.

The bandits' wagons yielded a hefty bounty of surplus, and some of it was extremely valuable—huge marquee cut diamonds and emeralds, the biggest Hungry had ever acquired. They spent a few hours digging through the wagons and gathering all the goods into two of them. Hungry also took the guns off a couple of the riders and stared in disbelief at their filthy faces, hats, and boots. He then piled the goods all in one wagon.

He took a minute to watch White Dove. She was always there to have his back, and she was so beautiful and deadly. They loaded up the carriages and started looking for horses who were scattered down the trail, some of them farther than others. A couple of them were alongside a little stream, saddled and easily approachable. They corralled them and took them back to the wagons just as they noticed more horsemen far in the distance. Indians—a war party or hunting party? They would soon find out.

Hungry and Dove quickly hitched up the team and prepared for whatever was next. They had extra rifles and pistols laid out along the floorboards of the stages. They pulled the coaches behind the big boulder, concealing them as well as they could, and sheltered the horses behind it. They climbed on top of the rocks, bringing as many rifles and pistols as they could, and set up for the shooting gallery.

The riders approached. They were definitely a war party—they had skinny white women tied to the back of a couple of their horses. They had paint on their faces—who knew what tribe they were from? Hungry knew they would not be able to talk or trade their way out of being killed, so he gestured to White Dove to use the rifles. They started with the .50 caliber and worked their way down to the 40s and 30s as the riders approached closer.

The Klamath—or whatever tribe they were—rode right into a thunderstorm. Bullets ripped apart the horsemen; chest pieces and flesh and bone fragments flew as the riders, once again, fell like tin soldiers brushed off of their metal horses by the wind.

Back in the state capital of Sacramento, another posse organized to scout out and bring back dead or alive Hungry Jack Hollow. This was the fifth organized ring of local deputized gunmen, Texas rangers, and sheriffs wanting to make a name for themselves. All were usually a rugged bunch good at gunfighting; most of them killed a few men, but every single one of them knew they were in for a gamble if they were going after Hungry and that he would be holding all of the aces.

The swaying long grass of the meadow and the cool breeze flowing down the canyon walls made it feel like one was going in slow motion, walking towards the evergreen vines and burrows. They looked up to the top of the cliffside but could still see no sign of their cabin or the trail that led them down to the meadow. The valley was vast and abundant, with deer, rabbits, and other small furry animals perfect for eating. They would hunt and set up drying stations to jerk their meats and preserve what they could for the cold winter.

It took a bitter cold to pierce Hungry's flesh, but he wondered if his White Dove had the same resistance. He also wondered about his buried treasures. Had anyone found entrances to the caves and made themselves to it? He knew he would have to go back and check for signs of trespassers.

He had left so much gold hidden because it was simply too heavy to carry around everywhere, and he only needed a saddle bag full to get anything he wanted in any county or town he had seen.

He came back to the realization that he was sitting on a rock next to a bubbling stream. White Dove was humming a tune that he had never quite heard before. She was naked in the swirling water—it tumbled from rounded dark rocks to surround her pale, slender body. It was a somber melancholy tone, slow and drawn out like a moan, but then slowly turning into a shrill, high-pitched, hawk-like scream. She ended her chant in a self-induced trance, slowly rising out of the water, with her body slightly twitching and her eyelids fluttering. Hungry didn't quite understand, but he did not have to pretend to enjoy it.

They spent hours in the water as it swirled around them, warm enough not to bring a chill but cool enough to keep them from sweating. They were alone in this valley as if they were the only two people alive on the planet. Animals did not seem to be afraid of them as they gathered their clothes and dressed on the water's edge.

Throughout the past couple of years, Hungry had built up a collection of high-grade, expensive cowboy boots: shiny, flashy ones, some black as coal, snakeskins, alligator, and a couple of different birds whose names he didn't even know—he just knew he liked them, and if they were his size he did not burn them. He might've built up such a liking for them watching so close- up as the gunfighters, gamblers, and cowboys walked along the boardwalks while he hid beneath as a child. He kept them all in his "lion cave," as he called it, one of his favorite caves.

In fact, it was where he had more than gold and guns and treasure buried: he had built an underground fortress and hide away, only a day's travel from their cabin. Would he dare take her there? Not quite yet; he would remain her companion for a while and decide if he could trust her enough to show her all of his treasures.

The first sign of her loyalty and trustworthiness came on a cold winter day when Jack was tracking a bear and checking his rabbit traps. He had become quite the trapper in the several months since he had met his White Dove, adorning her with furs and eating jerked rabbits, roasted deer meat, and boiled stews.

On this particular winter's day, he had fallen into an underground stream, breaking through thin ice, slicing his leg, and leaving him in quite a predicament. Once he realized that he was in a bad way, he immediately saw his White Dove. She must have sensed that he needed her because she seemed to be there instantly. He was nearly frozen when she pulled him out using a long tree branch that had broken off a nearby pine tree. She quickly made a fire and made a makeshift teepee out of only a few branches and some nearby pine needles and small twigs. All his rabbits were frozen along with all his furs as well as most of his legs. She rubbed it furiously, held him close to her chest, and returned the blood flow just in the nick of time to prevent him from certain frostbite.

I am born of worms I am born of worms I am born of worms I am born of worms I am born of worms I am born of worms I am born of warm.

Hungry came to sweating but was not cold anymore. He was comfortably surrounded by dry furs and hides of animals they had collected. She must have made it back to the hunter's cabin and back to him while he was unconscious. He was in another trapper's cabin located on the mountainside close to where he had broken through the ice miraculously. He had caught the pneumonia. The smell of her tobacco awakened him, and he realized that she cared for him. She seemed always smiling as she nursed him through his sickness while he grew stronger. It was the first time he had been wounded and felt cared for in so long. She had shown him care and affection before, but this was her giving him real honest commitment and… what was that word he had heard from Sunday church they sang about?

… Love?

It was another day of waning sunlight setting on a prehistoric spawn of rocks and mountains. The mountain range looked both giant and small at the same time. The purple skies looked painted, with reddish-orange splashes and golden-yellow streaks of twilight. Just about then, Hungry heard his horses. They were snorting, getting restless, and whiny.

He was able to stand and walk around again with a makeshift crutch and his leg wrapped up with a pine board. It seemed to be healing surprisingly fast. He moved to his gun depot and gathered his long rifles. He knew the trapper's cabin would be an easy target for bounty hunters, sheriff's possies, or bushwhackers. It was too out in the open to be a good hideout, so he rigged the tree line traps with a little extra something. As soon as he heard them gathering, he lit some fuses.

At first, the air went still and silent, and then the violent eruption of explosions occurred—it surrounded them and echoed intensely throughout the valley. Their ears were ringing. Men and horses were blown apart and buried in the rubble. This time, the air mostly smelled like sulfur and burning animal flesh. There was an occasional fresh pine scent when the wind would blow through. Some men were alive but had been dismembered. You could hear the faint screams of men and horses as they were lying on the blistered ground, blown to pieces. "I might have used too much," Hungry said out loud. The railroads stockpiled their explosive in little sheds that he would hijack and relocate. There was only one or two men moaning after the explosion. He sat down on the deck of the cabin and lit a smoke, hoping his ears would quit ringing and waiting to see if any of them could stand. After a few minutes, he moved in on the moaning and shot them in the chest with his pistol. He could see the shining tin metal of their broken stars—they were the sheriff's posse.

Luckily, they were the first ones to find him, he thought. They were usually the best gunmen. However, they were all torn to pieces. There must've been 13 or 14 of them, he gathered. He knew it was time to leave this valley and go back to his hideaway on the mountain's cliffside. White Dove approached him with extra gunnery, but he had already put the remaining out of their misery.

He gathered pieces of the dismembered bodies that looked like they went together and piled them together, sometimes putting arms where legs should go, sometimes putting their head where their crotch was. He wondered if this would make them stop chasing him. He didn't burn them; he left them for the vultures and wolves to feast. They gathered their supplies and slowly headed east toward the mountains.

Word got back to Sacramento about the horror the

sheriff's posse encountered. No one cared to join up for any posse for several years after that until some of the sons of the fallen lawmen—or one could say lawmen who were blown to pieces and not put back together again—came of age to avenge their dads.

After a few months of recuperating, Hungry decided to make the rounds and check his treasure hideouts. His leg was still kind of stiff but mostly healed. He had gold and jewels hidden all through the caves and hillsides of Auburn and the Middle Fork American River. One cavern was so vast it went completely under the river, branched out, and traveled downstream to areas filled with water that you would have to swim through. He decided it would be a safe place for them to go, and he trusted White Dove enough to show her everything he had. He was lucky to have escaped that trapper's cabin. They made their way, on foot, through the valley, and along the rocky-edged cliff paths until they came to the tunnels of the American River.

It was like a second home to him. He loved the smell of the musty earth and the damp air of the tunnel. Hungry had explored all parts of this tunnel system as a child and a young adult. He would spend days camping in the caverns, hiding his gold and treasures. He stayed in the upper end of the tunnels, which was devoid of a natural water source but still humid. The damp air relaxed him as he dug out the areas that were entrances to other chambers he had sealed up. Some of them went to side tunnels, and some were hidden in the ceilings covering his head. He would stand back as the dirt, wooden boards, and rocks would tumble down, revealing an opening to another cave system that was completely hidden. They would travel through it and uncover more hidden doorways to finally get to his favorite hiding place.

Chapter 5

The Crystal Cave

Several crates of gold and gunnysacks of coins and jewels were hidden in each cave, but this cave had a special energy to it. It always seemed to rejuvenate and make him think clearly.

He rummaged through his treasures of gold and jewelry and could tell instantly that no one had been there since the last visit. He realized he had brought her to his sacred, secret place. He wondered if she knew she was the only one with whom he had shared his collections of treasure and gold. Would she murder him in his sleep and take it and run? He was willing to take the chance.

He took her to the back of the cavern and showed her his collection of diamonds, rubies, and emeralds. He had a secret rock that blocked a passageway in the side of a tunnel that you could barely squeeze through; you would have to slide down a tube of red clay dirt to come into another open room about as big as a train car.

He had carved out shelves along the edge of the room and placed candles in there for illumination. He had adorned it with all his treasures of silver, gold, emeralds, rubies, and more. On the side opposite side of the room, where he had built a wooden shelf, he kept his cowboy boots, some with shiny buckles, others black as bat wings. They were all kept neat, stacked in fruit boxes, and wrapped in burlap. He would sit there alone all the time, wondering which ones he should wear; this was the first time he had shared it with anyone.

White Dove was in disbelief. She had never seen so much gold and treasure and could not imagine what they could even do with it all. She was content with her cabin hidden in the mountain's cliffside and the life of hunting with Hungry. She even enjoyed hunting the bad people and the ones that tried to attack them.

But this was like being in a dream to her. The air had an alien tinge to it that she had never smelt. The water trickled down the rocks at the lower end of the room and gathered in two little pools that spilled out through the cracks on the bottom of the floor. Crystals of gold, purple, and blue shined through the ripples… tiny tentacles of mist rose from the water as it passed over the crystals. This place was a truly magical natural beauty adorned with man-made treasure.

They spent hours there exploring all the different items Hungry had acquired throughout his explorations and plundering. He had the tools of the trade of every tradesman, and he had dentistry and medical equipment. He had new inventions frontier men had carried west to San Francisco to become mass-produced. He acquired all this through his outlaw travels and kept it with the other treasure the cave had to offer.

He had not acquired any female garments. Hungry preferred her to be naked anyway. He smiled as he dug out an old steamer trunk and revealed its furs and animal pelts. Some were all white, mostly from white foxes, rabbits, and snow leopards. He handed them to her, knowing she would love them. He said, "For you." Hungry was entranced by her beauty as she revealed her naked body to the candlelight; it was his finest treasure, he thought to himself. Her long, slender body had curves in all the right places. She looked at him with both eyes shining and repeated his words back to him, "For you."

Morning came, and they found themselves on the outside ledge near the cave's entrance, except you could not tell it was a cave anymore. Hungry always hid it with giant rocks and dirt he used for mortar to fill the gaps. He even replaced them with moss and green sprouts of weeds so that any travelers passing by would not take a second glance. They were usually always on cliffsides where you were trying to look down to make sure you made it through the trail. The sun crested the jagged, rocky mountain tops as buzzards circled throughout the sunrise in several spots along the valley below. Feeding time came early for these birds.

Hungry knew he had to beat it back to flatland. He wondered if his new side companion would be okay with some more killing, for just about anyone you came upon on these back trails was either looking to rob you or bring you to the law for a date with the hangman's noose. He woke up his White Dove and suggested that they go up the mountain, saying a couple of simple words and pointing "up the mountain." She replied, smiling, "We go." They had bagged up some of the supplies and stuff they wanted out of the cave for now. He wrapped her white fur in burlap for her before they sealed up all the caves. They worked their way along the narrowing edge of the riverbank and climbed up rock ledges and hills to then ascend into valleys past rattlesnakes and lizards that just seemed to stare at them from jagged rock outcroppings, like normal reptiles of their kind. They continued on for hours until dropping their way back down to find a lake and bathed in it.

Every time Hungry left the cave, he felt a curious energy glowing inside him. He became more aware of his surroundings and faster at slinging iron. He had first found that cave as a boy. He remembered going there after trailing some robbers and stealing the loot that they hid there. He just took their loot farther back into the cave and buried it again.

He was good at digging and hiding things. He would wait several months before going back to get his loot, and in those several months, he had matured ten times the amount of a normal boy. After returning, he would retrieve only part of his gold, and then he would go back. He felt the crystal cave gave him everlasting power.

Hungry wondered if White Dove had the same reaction. It was her first time in the caves, and they went far to the back. Her eyes seemed to grow a little wider, and her smile was brighter. His leg was not stiff any longer. He was curious about what she was going to do with the tiny jewels and medical supplies that she asked him to take. There were some jewels the size of green figs and plums, yet she chose the ones hardly bigger than a fire ant or bug.

He liked bugs. He had watched how flies and other flying creatures formed from white worms. He would witness their metamorphosis and watch them fly away from the piles of garbage, crap, or dead animal that they came from; that's most likely why he didn't mind the few that swarmed around him in his younger years.

White Dove stared at him with admiration. She loved the way his face was half-frightening and half-boyish-warrior. He was so quick-witted and fast-thinking; he was always a step ahead of her. She let him be without resistance. He had saved her so many times, but he was not a good swimmer like her, so she kept an eye on him in the water like a mother hen.

They gathered their clothes and continued towards the

trail that led to the higher ground. The rocky landscape gradually sloped uphill as they traveled; the wind blew in, carrying the scent of pine tree needles and wildflowers as they continued on their travels. They were feeling refreshed and content on their journey to the higher elevation. It wasn't long before they encountered trouble; several riders, with their horses, circled, hooting and hollering and shooting their guns off from behind some rocks. As Hungry and White Dove approached, they could tell they were outlaws. Gunfighting gamblers who win, lose, or draw always robbed, shot up the town, and headed to the high ground carrying their loot.

Hungry thought to himself, *"I'm already loaded down with guns, supplies, and gold; what am I gonna do with more guns and gold?"* He silently walked past their makeshift encampment just as they broke up their meeting. The bandits fast mounted their horses and started riding towards Hungry and Dove. They both quickly hid off their trail, tucked themselves deep back into the manzanita bushes, and let all of the riders pass. Hungry looked at White Dove. She was smiling, playfully signaling him to get more tobacco while whispering the word "tobacco." He said to her, "We'll follow quietly." They proceeded to trail the horsemen, staying back far enough not to be heard, following them on foot, quietly but steadily, to see where they were going.

Checking his back trail often, he realized there were also

several men on horseback following them now up the canyon. Following the fugitives and being caught between the law and the outlaws, Hungry was finally starting to feel a little adrenaline like he used to feel when he would have a shootout or knife fight at a saloon. All of the railroad men, lawmen, gunmen, and other men of leadership would seem to like poking fun at him as a kid. So he, too, had a strong hatred for any type of authority figure and wasn't that fond of them being anywhere near him. They all were kind of heartless, self-concerned individuals that usually started the fight. He took pleasure in killing them. He would most likely kill this gang of lawmen first. Hungry was thinking about the town saloons; he did want to take his White Dove for a night in town.

Hungry and White Dove walked and ran in the shadows of the rocks and the recesses of the trail, rocks lining the edges of the main road. They traveled at about the same speed with the same interval between them for miles. They could see the valley below, but to leave the trail would mean getting spotted by one side or the other.

After a couple of miles, Hungry realized he would have to take out the horsemen in the rear. It would be good if he could do it silently without gunfire. He kept his eyes open for the perfect overhead boulder to take out a few of them and ruin the trail for further passengers.

It didn't take long. There were several jagged rocks above 15 or 20 feet of loose dirt rounding around the outside of the mountain. He and Dove scurried up the deer trail that went straight up the mountain. She followed him like a wild cat. They didn't even have to hide their tracks because they didn't leave any. Loose dirt slid over any track they made as they continued upward. Then, they silently made their way around to the backside of the rocks just above the trail. There were three or four slabs of large rocks cracked loose, so they put their back to the center one and waited for the sound of horses, hooves, or even men on their feet.

The riders were a quiet bunch; one almost passed the slide zone before Hungry heard the sound of hooves on stone and motioned for White Dove to help him push. They pushed the loose giant slab of rock over at the perfect moment to start a small earth slide that took out the first few riders. The two that were left just seemed to look at each other for a moment in amazement.

The bottom of the cliff below was only about 40 feet, but the landing was not soft; part of the trail started to fall away in clouds of dust as you could hear the crunch of bones against rocks and the drone of screams fast-lived and ending even faster. The surviving lawmen looked at the bottom of the mountainside in horror after staring at each other in disbelief. They had clearly seen the huge rock sliding down the mountain, but they didn't act to have seen any sign of

Hungry or White Dove. They turned and headed down the trail the other way and glanced up once again at where Hungry and White Dove recessed into a crevice of another cracked rock, but unless they had seen them and were pretending otherwise, they went unnoticed. Hungry judged that, by their reactions, they appeared to not have seen either of them.

It was highly possible that the surviving lawmen likely just figured they were in the back part of the mountains where one could encounter rock slides, outlaws that out number you, or possibly even Indians. They were making a trail out of there. If it were Indians, it was usually an entire war party rather than a few individual warriors that you would encounter. The Maidu Indians ruled much of the land and parts of the mountains he was about to pass through.

He remembered the medicine man who was always kind to him. The man had helped him heal his face when the dog attacked him. Hungry had killed many dogs after that; he had kind of lost interest in that now. He knew that he kicked the dog too much, but it was just always stealing his food, so he would sometimes beat it before it had a chance to. Sometimes, he was a little extra mean. He was going to see how much the other members of the posse meant to the two surviving lawmen. They waited for close to an hour after hearing them leave before he peered out with White Dove. They stood together and admired the carnage, lit up a smoke to share, and watched the trail for a little longer.

After reassuring himself that surviving lawmen had probably gone back to Sacramento, which was a one or two-day journey on a fast horse, they went down the rockslide to the flat ledge below to see what was left of the riders. The boulders had taken out a couple of them, completely smashing their bodies into puddles of flesh and blood leaking from under flat slabs of giant stone. Some were just pinned and suffering. One man had a broken arm with a bone sticking out of his forearm and half his face scraped off; he was quietly praying. They disarmed the ones that were alive, took their guns, and shot their horses—they were suffering badly anyway.

Before leaving, Hungry carved out some nice horse steaks to jerk and cook on the next campfire. They smoked the lawmen's tobacco. One was blue, bludgeoned, and bleeding profusely out of his ear, and you could see his jaw had been cracked sideways. His tongue was so swollen from biting half of it off. He looked a mess, so Hungry calmly shot him between the eyes and put him out of his suffering. He was really not coming out of that one, but his companion, who was alive with a broken arm, had a good chance. He would be the first survivor of Hungry's homicidal travels that he did not kill. The man was not rude to him, only thankful, even after Hungry had killed his companions. He knew he was a goner.

Hungry left him there after freeing his arm. He left the injured man a horse but kept his guns and shiny brass badge for one of his treasures. Of course, he took all their gold, silver, pocket watches, knives, and containers. One of them had a worthy pair of cowboy boots. Two of the bodies were crushed under a giant boulder. That huge boulder had been at the bottom of the rockslide reaction and caught them perfectly. Their boots were still perfect, though.

He did not forget their tobacco. They both realized riders from the outlaw gang of lead horsemen were coming back down the trail to investigate the noise from the gunshots and rock slide. As soon as the horsemen rounded the corner, they were greeted by arrows and bullets. It was a gun battle. Hungry and White Dove crouched behind the fallen boulders and started target practice. They were blasting holes in the hats and heads of all the riders as they approached. Dove was shooting them with arrows in the neck and face. They were not on fire this time—just accurate and fast. The gunmen got a few shots off before slumping in their saddles and sliding down their horses like melted horsemen. The shootout only lasted a few seconds. At least now, they could move forward on good mounts with an extra amount of horsepower to carry all their newfound guns and loot.

The bandit crew of four had done quite well in their looting of a Wells Fargo stagecoach. They had one box of gold that had already damn near killed the horse that was carrying it. Hungry let that horse go and mounted the box onto a giant, black Clydesdale. It was the horse the lead bandit had been riding. He rolled the bodies down the rock slide to be with their chasers and the one they left. He would take the glory, but who would tell the true story? This was a warning message to others to stay away from these mountain trails.

Chapter 6
Rubies And Diamonds

Hungry and White Dove continued on their path. It was rather peaceful after the aftermath of their last encounter. The horses seemed to like them more compared to their previous riders, who had ridden them to the point of exhaustion.

The afternoon breeze blew somberly. The sky was a brilliant blue with white clouds and streaks of silver. They came upon a crosspath in the trail. Bones of animals like bulls, cows, and longhorns lined the intersection of the trail. They continued north towards the path of the ravine and kept an eye out for cave entrances to hide the Wells Fargo box.

He was thinking about the old stagecoach robber that he met; he was another man Jack held in high regard. "'Black Bart,' they called him," he explained to White Dove. The bandit, like himself, would also write poetry. He would leave the letters for all to read after he would make his way off with the gold box. He robbed stagecoaches, but he was not a killer. Hungry had been so busy with his new friend and companion that he had not written or recited any poetry. Instead, he had been living it in a way.

A few miles along the trail, they found the place where

the mountain changed to rocks with giant surfaces. There were a couple of cave entrances right off the main trail, but they continued a little further to find one hidden a little better that was farther off the main trail.

They entered the cave carefully at first—it could be the lair of a mountain lion or a bear. It was a narrow entry going down diagonally towards an opening where there could be an animal waiting. Hungry went first with two of his knives in front of him. He knew better than to shoot guns in a cave, as he'd seen the outcome of that one before. This one was empty, luckily, so he hurried back to the horses and settled all the surplus to the mouth of the cave.

He could barely move the gold box, so he walked the horse as close as he could to the entrance and slid it off his back. With the help of White Dove, they got it through the opening and worked it to the back of the cave. It was a perfect bench for them to sit on as they lit some candles and took a minute to get comfortable.

Hungry went back to the trail, gathered the horses there, unbridled them, took off their saddles, and sent them on their way. The presence of horses would have been an easy giveaway, even if they made traveling a lot more practical. After they were gone, he took a pine branch, brushed away any tracks, and returned to the cave.

He found White Dove playing with the diamonds and

rubies she had collected. She was melting gold and silver together to make an electro-metal and forming tiny strips of it to showcase and hold the jewels. She had the dental supplies spread out next to her and a cracked sliver of a mirror stuck in the wall where she looked at herself. She motioned for Hungry to come sit by her and look in the mirror. He was bashful to look at his left side and his upper missing lip. She shook her head and made him look at it in the mirror.

She held up the fastened diamond and ruby pieces laced with metal that she had placed in the perfect position to fit around Hungry's revealed upper teeth. She knew he liked fancy things and shiny metal. The way the light reflected off the facets of the diamonds and rubies made his wicked smile shine with an aristocratic air. He liked the shimmering red and silver colors it brought to his smile. It made him look very wicked when he grimaced, too.

She took some more of the supplies, filed spots on his teeth, mixed powders and glues, and made them permanent, removing some of his rotten spots. It was painful, but the pain only lasted a day. He gazed at his reflection in the jagged shard of mirrored glass and thought... he had really come a long way since he had found a way to escape his life's past unpleasantries, just like the fly born of a worm only to change mysteriously and grow wings and fly. He decided to show off the new mouth jewels. He put on his newest cowboy boots and his new sheriff star and prepared to take her to the town saloon for a little drinking and dancing. They gathered some supplies and started to head towards the lights of the town. Lucky for them, the big black Clydesdale was still resting not far away on the trail.

Hungry had not been to the town for a couple of years, at least not this town. Penryn, they called it. You could usually see its firelight from the mountain above at nightfall. They traveled northwest until they finally lost sight of the Sierra Mountains and left the rocky-towered pathways to travel on more rolling dirt hills with only some rocks and caves.

Hungry had jewels hidden in a cave on their route. He was surprised that White Dove had picked the small jewels out for him and that she wanted nothing for herself. He felt her grip on his hips as she straddled his, and they rode bareback.

The skyline was cobalt blue and purple, with the orange-red trails of a fiery sunset. They came to the ravine and rode through the long flowing wheatgrass meadows toward the saloon in Penryn. It was completely dark when they drew close to town. You could hear some laughter and occasional screams and gunfire. The smell of cattle assaulted their nose as they came upon a cattle camp just on the outskirts of town. They walked their horse into town and set it loose—*"This time, it would know to stick around,*" Jack thought to himself as Dove whispered something into its ear.

They walked the remaining distance to the small town— one mercantile, one post office, and a saloon... no sheriff's office. They just hung you or shot you if you got into trouble with the law in this camp town. The saloon air was full of tobacco smoke. It also smelled of old beer. It was bustling with activity: gambling gunmen, dancing girls, women for the night, and cowboys. Glasses were being refilled, and bottles were being emptied. An endless supply of different kinds of alcohol aligned on the shelves above the bar, reflecting the colors of a rainbow in the dim lights.

He caught his reflection in the mirror-backed shelf between the Mexican tequila and whiskey bottle. He had first noticed a worm in the bottle, but then he saw the gleam of the diamonds and ruby that looked like a natural feature of his mouth. Now his teeth looked whiter, and the shiny metal and gems made him look a little like he had removed his lip so you could see it.

He looked back to see his White Dove. She was eating peanuts and pointing at a bar glass. He took in all the patrons of the bar, the ceiling lights, and the parlor rooms upstairs, and at first, nobody paid them any notice. He told the bartender to get a whiskey sour for two, and he purchased some tailor-made cigarettes from a salesman and handed them over to White Dove. She was quietly still and acted like she was trying not to be seen. She still had the white garments and seashell bracelets on, her high-top moccasins were still pure white, and she was as thin as a rail. Her bow and knife never left her side, but she had hidden most of her arrows under the walking boards in the darkness of the night before she entered the bar. She lit up a smoke and blew smoke rings in the face of the barman who still would not serve her.

The barkeep stared in disbelief at her. Grimacing, Hungry replied by slapping the barman and asking for two glasses, a bottle of their finest whiskey, and that juice flask *again*. He looked at Hungry and went straight for his shotgun under the counter. Hungry reacted fast with one of his long knives. He placed it right through the back of the barman's neck as he bent over to reach the gun. The barkeep grunted, and the air left his body. The tip of the blade came out of his mouth a little; blood and saliva ran down it as his lungs filled with fluids, and he sank to the ground.

Hungry instantly climbed behind the bar and mixed his drinks into the canteen: 3/4 whiskey and 1/4 lime. He slid it down the bar to White Dove. She put it around her neck, locked in the one arrow she brought into the bar, and stood next to Hungry. It took a minute for the crowd to realize what was happening. Several armed cattlemen rushed the bar, and one screamed, "That was old Dick, you bastard!"

They were going for their guns when Hungry's bullets pierced their faces and hearts. He shot the head clean off one of them with the bar's shotgun and then emptied six bullets from each of his pistols in a split second. He thought to himself, *"I'm getting quicker at this."*

White Dove was truly impressed. She had kept her arrow notched but never had time to pick a target. Hungry had cleaned the floor. Most of the people left except for the piano player, a few gamblers, and the dancing girls. Hungry opened the bar to them, offering whiskey sours, and they continued their activities as if nothing happened. A man came out of the back and dragged the bodies away, rolling the head like a bowling ball with his foot, sprinkling peanut shells on the ground, and muttering to himself.

The piano man struck up a tune, and it actually had some life to it. The lights seemed to get a little brighter as the tobacco and gunfire smoke left the room. There, in the piped coal gas-lit bar room, they looked at each other and smiled wide, taking a swig from their canteens. Hungry reloaded his guns and laid them out on the bar table facing the doors. He collected the rest of the firearms and checked them for bullets. They would stay for a few more songs, he figured, before they would have to head out of town fast.

Hungry looked at White Dove and smiled. She still remained silky white and clean—white as the worms the flies were born from, white like the birds of the ocean. His mouth jewels gleamed like flames of fire, each in the perfect position to highlight the other. His shiny black Stetson hat set it off, framing his wicked, thin features. The Stetson hat company came out when he was only twelve. His mother used to tell him that it was the only hat a man should wear. She had saved one of the first ones for him until he was thirteen—that's when he also got his first guns from her. He had pistols, knives, and cowboy hats way before that, though. At six, he would butcher his own meat.

They watched the crowd begin to gather again. No one looked at them. He started looking around the place. In a side room, he found the kitchen with the smell of meat and herbs coming from it. Sure enough, there were a couple of cooks with steaks of some sort on the fire. He had them prepare some for them, including a full leg of beef for the road and half of one for the moment. They stayed a while longer, and Hungry ate enough for five men. He drank, and they danced to the piano man's happy and sad jingles, all the while keeping an eye on the windows and front door. They refilled their canteens with the finest whiskey, gathered their new guns and gold, and slid out the back door.

They encountered no resistance, and White Dove was able to collect her hidden arrows. Apparently, all the lawmen and gunmen of the town had been in the bar that particular night and had been either killed by Hungry or had never come down from upstairs. There, in the tree line, stood the Clydesdale stallion, looming like a mythical giant silhouetted by the full moon. The sky had turned to deep purples and dark blues. It churned slices of white crystalline clouds into its canopy. They mounted the horse with their new supplies and headed back towards the hills and the town of Lincoln. It had been the time of life for the both of them, and Hungry actually felt like he wasn't starving for an hour or two.

As they passed the cattle camps and headed into the darkness, they could hear the distant war cries of the Maidu Indian's hunting party. They were moving in their direction with caution. It was odd that no one seemed to be awake in the camps they passed as they followed the now-moonlit trail. They crossed the ravine and headed up the grade. They stopped to rest for the night on the high ledge of a canyon at a giant granite rock pile with a vulture's nest in the highest peaks of rocks. Skeletons of animals and other small bones encircled the nest; it was empty at the moment. She was not happy with the nest so close to them—empty or not. She started remembering how she was hunting for food with her bow and quiver of arrows when she saw two quail. When she shot, her arrows missed. She ate part of the mushroom and later passed out. Luckily, she came to before the vultures picked her apart.

There were three of them: one pecking a hole in her

belly that just started pulling out strings of belly muscle, the other one was on her neck trying to rip away some skin and flesh, and the third was pecking at her eye—it had ripped off most of her upper eyelid as she violently woke up. The birds were vicious; they didn't stop until she stabbed them and twisted their necks with her bare hands. She was in her own wild frenzy, covered with blood; bird feathers were in the air being swirled around in the wind. She remembered their stink of rotten flesh and death and could only see red out of the wounded eye. It was a little traumatizing for her.

She lit the nest on fire with her perfume bottle lighter, and Hungry looked at her through the crackling yellow-orange and red flames and smiled wide, his diamonds and rubies capturing and reflecting the dancing flames in their facets. They drank whiskey from their canteens and looked at the fire, watching the last sparks and embers of nest twigs blowing in the wind. Then, they walked farther along the trail leading up the ravine until they came to another one of Hungry's hideouts.

The moon had moved out of sight by the time they reached that cave opening. They had to dig out a giant boulder and roll it out of the second opening. It was not much bigger than a wagon tire, but it was heavier than it looked. They were dead tired and stayed out of the cave to listen for any other signs of life; the small trail leading to the cave was just big enough for their horse to stand. If anyone came along, they would surely be alerted.

They all slept well that night. White Dove stayed just inside the entrance of the cave after Hungry checked it out for any animal intruders. He kissed her neck and ate several beef steaks from the saloon kitchen, then stayed close to her for the remainder of the night with his shotguns and pistols loaded next to the cave's entrance. There was a rabbit den in which they would hunt and eat its residents in the morning. As he closed his eyes to the night, he thought of the treasure he had in the cave. It was his lion's den, where he had hidden so much gold and jewelry. He had his cowboy hats and boots, his Stetsons, and jewelry from past queens of distant countries. He remembered a huge clear diamond neckpiece that he would look for in the morning.

In this cave, Hungry had mirrors set up to reflect the morning light back into the deep chambers of the walls. He had found a sleeping mountain lion in this cave when he had first entered it some ten years back. He thought to himself, *"That creature was surely magnificent,"* as he faded to sleep.

The sunlight's warmth brought a radiant energy to the cave. The moss on the rocks threw little columns of steam that followed the cave's walls to their arches. Light shafts reflected throughout the cave, lighting up stained glass bottles and vases of the Ming dynasty's era. There they stood, surrounded by all of Hungry's treasure of gold, silver, guns, and knives. He moved some hatboxes to uncover an oak wooden jewelry box with a special hidden lock that you needed long fingers or a strong stick to open. At first, he was going to give her the huge clear diamond in it, but then he decided to give her the whole box. It had gemstones of every color and held almost every different kind of valuable mineral or stone. Each section was removable and placed into showcase boxes so you could pick one up, unlock it if desired, and hold it to the light to see the reflected colors that each made.

The box was about as big as a hatbox, but it was thick wood, and it was tricky to open, so he handed it to her and said it was a puzzle. She repeated the word "puzzle" and looked at him. Over the month, they had communicated more with words than with hand signals. They could almost always read each other's thoughts and had developed their own style of secret language. Her skin was extremely pale sometimes, and her blue eyes would turn an ice-white blue in certain situations.

He had seen an albino deer before—it was like her, magical and rare to encounter. He set it down and showed her the trick to opening the box. She didn't take long to figure it out, and when the necklace unraveled itself to her, it was like a glowing firestone, glimmering with sparks and energy. She had seen rings and fine necklaces made of this stone but never anything like this. It was the same type of crystal she had made his teeth jewels with.

He put it around her neck and said the word "diamond." It weighted her neck down; the chain was white gold, but they didn't care much. She admired the stone's beauty and the glimmer of rainbows that shone through its faucets. She knew she could not carry this around and asked if she could keep it with the rest of his stuff. He gave White Dove her own corner and filled it with gold, coins, guns, and knives. He had a ceremonial willow tree bow and some red Obsidian tipped arrows from an Indian tracker that he had kept after killing him and the posse he had been in. He gave it to her as well.

She was in awe and didn't know how to accept so many gifts. Again, she could be instantly wealthy if she wanted to sell these, but she had grown to really love the companionship, adventure, and danger that Hungry had brought to her life. He had put on one of his newest hats and sets of boots. These boots were made of alligator skin, and they had shiny silver Italian made spurs. He normally didn't wear spurs because they jingled when you walked and made too much noise.

He went outside of the cave to check some rabbit traps and check his back trail. Gunfire interrupted him, and it wasn't something small—it sounded to be at least .50

caliber, repeating like a war drum. Rocks were exploding next to the cave entrance. His beautiful black Clydesdale horse was blown into pieces right in front of him, and its blood and insides covered the trail. Slowly, the horse's bullet-severed body fell off the cliff to the ground below, leaving bright red blood-streaked trails over the edge. Hungry quickly backed into the cave and took off his spurs and boots. He motioned for Dove to get back farther into the cave.

Chapter 7

The Gatlin Gun

As he told her, she knew what was going on: someone from the last town had called the army, or it was another sheriff posse—someone with a fast-repeating giant gun. Hungry moved fast and, using the boulder for cover, rolled it back in front of the cave entrance. He did not know if they had seen the cave, but as soon as he got it covered with the boulder, he heard the ground erupt with gunfire again. He then looked at his White Dove and loudly said the words "Gatling gun" to her.

Several small cave-ins were happening along the front of the passageway, and where the boulder had been visible was now completely covered in dirt and smaller rocks that fell from above. No light remained in the tunnel. The cave was pitch black until White Dove lit an arrow with her perfume bottle. The firelight flickered along the damp cave walls. The blasting stopped after another minute, and it was so silent you could hear a hat pin drop.

Hungry found some candles, lit them, and set them up in places all around. He had dried foods and canned meat, and there was a little water in one of the passageways. This was a big cave system with plenty of air, so he was not too worried at the moment. They concentrated on loading all their guns and placing them facing the now caved-in entry. All of a sudden, their days had changed to nights. Inside the cave, they would lose track of days, not knowing if it was night or day outside.

Hungry thought about his horse. Seeing it ripped to pieces with huge bullets made him mad as hell. He was tempted to dig out and confront them, but he did not even know if they knew he was in there. They listened quietly for a long time before starting to dig their way to that rock at the entrance.

After a couple of days of being isolated, they had eaten most all of their food and were tired of the cave. They had looked at all the jewelry and gold coins, and their candles were burning short. Hungry reached the rock and almost had it dug out when another cave-in trapped half of his body in it. White Dove was there to help dig them out in an instant, but he did get a little broken up. His fingers on his left hand and the side of his right arm were all scraped up and smashed pretty badly.

He made his way back to the water and washed off his wounds. There were small scraps of food that White Dove had collected that they nibbled on and drank the last of their whiskey while they waited another day or two for Hungry's wounds to heal. They put their candles out to preserve them and would just hold each other in the darkness like vampires in a sarcophagus waiting out the daylight to rise and feast on the living. They explored each other's bodies in the dark on a bed of furry pelts, animal hides, and skins. The dank earth scent of the cave surrounded their senses, and they were neither hot nor cold.

They made shoring out of wooden crates to hold up the dirt, roots, and small rocks lodged in the roof of the tunnel. This time, when they dug their rabbit hole out, they would be safe. They were digging for about half a day before they reached an opening. With the sound of grunting and falling rocks and moving earth, they emerged into the night. Stars were shining like jewels on a black velvet canvas. There was a silver moon lying on a blanket of white clouds. An owl called out in the night, but all else was quiet as they lay there, breathing in the fresh air and being thankful they made it out alive.

It must've been close to a week that they were in that cave, and there were no signs of any of the ambushers. The carcass of the horse had been picked clean by wolves and buzzards. There were tracks of up to 14 or 15 men, plus carriage tracks and bullet cartridges of all sizes. They shot a lot of rounds off; whoever was after them clearly thought they had killed them. They blasted half of the mountain away and started a small avalanche that blocked part of the trail. No one could have withstood that volley of gunfire. They must've not seen the second cave. Hungry and White Dove were on foot now, but they still followed tracks until they started to lead back to the cow camp near Penryn. They made a hideout in the tree line beside some large granite boulders with some branches and pine needles.

Hungry killed and cleaned a smaller cow and cut it up into steaks and strips of meat for jerking. He found a safe spot to make a fire and started cooking. They ate half of the calf, with Hungry eating like he had not had food for a month. His hand was better; luckily, he had just scraped everything really badly, and there were no broken bones. He could still fire a weapon with it, although his right hand was much faster now.

He brought his meat back to the shelter, and they ate while they kept an eye on the cattle town. The next day, the wagon train and the 14 or 15 gunmen all headed west. They were done looking for him and headed toward Sacramento. They looked like soldiers or lawmen of some sort. He had seen a couple of stars and metals on their vest. It was time for him to take the hunt to them. He had never had a Gatling gun, he thought to himself.

They followed on their tracks foot, staying far enough away not to be seen. They traversed up and down the mountains' rocky faces to save time and catch them at the canyon's basin. It was quite a task catching up with their horses and carriages, but they were both fury-driven by the way their attackers had almost blown them into pieces like the beautiful black Clydesdale they had been riding. After a couple day journey they caught sight of the posse. They had taken time to camp and drink along the river's winding trail. Hungry had already picked out the horse he liked—it was a giant white one. The rider was unkind to it; he was an extremely large man and it would not be hard to shoot him right off of it.

Hungry observed. He wanted to start blasting them off of their horses, but they followed and waited for nightfall to settle. It was about dark when they got to the outskirts of Sacramento. The sky above was dark blue and black, with pinpoints of starlight. There was a vivid skyline of low-pressure clouds blowing in from the west, shining white with purples and reds rippling like waves. They followed the river and ended up on a sandy barge just around the river bend.

The group of men made camp. They stood by the campfire and congratulated each other while drinking and smoking. They were talking about how they were going to the cat house before entering the town in the morning. They laughed and left the two behind that drew the shortest straws. They would have to wait for relief before they could go into town.

As soon as they were to themselves, the two riders left behind to watch the camp started making wild animal noises and signs on the wagon cover, using their hands and making images of dogs, crocodiles, and birds appear. These were some silly bastards, Hungry thought as he pointed to the one by the fire. White Dove let arrows fly, striking each of them in the neck. The first cattleman stumbled into the firepit and went down, his hat, vest, and face quickly burning in the red and orange flames. The other was turning in circles, holding on to the arrow lodged in his throat, completely falling sideways as his legs spread wider. Hungry quickly moved in and sliced him from ear to ear. He made a gurgling noise and kicked his feet a lot. Hungry tossed him in the fire pit also. The air started smelling like burning flesh and charred leather.

It was all over in a matter of a minute. They were pulling the smoldering bodies out of the fire and away from the stagecoach to hide them behind a manzanita brush pile. There were several horses, and a team was still connected to the wagon with the Gatling gun. It seemed to be made of mostly polished brass. Hungry shuffled all the supplies into that wagon, all the bullets and gunpowder he could fit, and they quickly collected the white stallion, and Dove mounted it. It seemed to know her instantly. Hungry drove his new team off the road into the darkness of the night, leaving behind the river of Sacramento and heading back for the trail towards the city of Auburn, established in 1848. Then they traveled back down through its canyons, twists, and turns to the American rivers and the perfect caves to hide his new weapon.

Would the rest of the posse or Calvary catch up with them before that, or would they stay at the whore houses all night, leaving the two guards out in the cold? That's what Hungry was betting on. He knew if you got left behind when the others went into town, you were there until morning. He had watched plenty of gun hands of all varieties, and they always made the weaker minds do the worst and hardest chores. So he took extra time, making tracks that led to different places to throw them off his trail. He knew that he would get the better of them in a gun battle for sure now that he had the Gatling gun.

They took time out of the day to figure out how to fire it from the top of a ridge. You had to lay the bands of bullets just perfectly so they would rotate along the track into position. The crank handle was almost too hard for White Dove, but she gave it a few turns with Hungry's help. They held off firing it too much; they kept moving through the night until they found the perfect area behind some rocks to wait for the rest of them.

It was only about half a day before they heard horse hooves striking the ground and felt the rumble of many riders approaching. White Dove moved to a lower vantage point where she had a tree line and several down trees for her cover. They patiently waited for the posse to approach. Their tactics worked perfectly—the squad of army men, cattlemen, and lawmen entered fast on horseback. They didn't spread out, but there were a couple that hung back. Hungry noticed that they all suddenly slowed their approach. It was an obvious open shooting range; once you entered and were close enough, there was nowhere to hide except behind your horse.

They were already at the threshold when flaming arrows started finding their targets. The three lead riders slumped over. One caught a bullet between the eyes, and the other had a flaming arrow go through his heart. They drew closer to the area where the wagon was covered. Hungry quickly ran to the wagon, pulled back the canvas, and started cranking the handle of the Gatling gun. He swung the barrel in the direction of the riders as the bullets ripped them to pieces— horses, saddles, riders, none were a match to the .50 caliber bullets rapidly flying through the air and taking them into oblivion, shredding them into pieces. This was an awesome piece of machinery.

Even though his arm was about to give in, he kept on cranking. He had taken down every last rider, leaving them in pieces shredded by its .50 caliber ammunition. Hungry just about entirely disintegrated the giant lead man by continually firing on his carcass. He let the silence prevail and stood there in awe after witnessing the wrath of his Gatling gun. It was truly exquisite, and he would make sure he would take it somewhere to be preserved and ready for use again when he needed it.

This was pretty much the end of his struggle with that posse. He realized they had almost cost him his life. Luckily, he had dug his way out of the cave and they had enough food and water to sustain their life for the days they were buried. These hell-bent fools had now paid. Their bodies were ripped to pieces, and their horses were also shredded, giant piles of carcasses that would soon be feeding the wolves, coyotes, mountain lions, and buzzards. Hungry knew that he had to step up his game—this had been a close call.

Hungry took a horse and scouted for more riders on their back trail. After he was completely satisfied there were no more lawmen he moved onward with his covered wagon and his new white stallion. They would go to the caves at the north and south rivers of the Americans and hide all of their loot and the Gatling gun. After, they would cut a trail to Lincoln. He still wanted to show her a night on the town where he was born.

The Gatling gun was invented in 1861, and this had to be one of the first ones ever made. He was definitely proud of this treasure, and he would take it to the cave where they had stayed once before—the Crystal Cave. They journeyed for a few days through pine tree forests and along rocky ledges until, finally, they came closer to the Great American

River bank and the cave's first entrance.

The cavern had several caves that, once inside their entry spots and hidden rock doors, led to giant tunnels. The entry was hidden also by giant boulders amid pine trees. It was a common-looking cave until you went back several yards, and it had some twisting down tunnels. Some tunnels completely went under the river, so you could come up on the other side. It was here that the tunnel turned upward also, and the carriage stopped just in time not to make the horses slide down the vertical shaft.

It was getting dark again, and there was no moon in the sky. It wasn't the first time he hid an entire wagon. He backed the wagon up to a wider part of the opening, unleashed the horses, and let them run back free, hoping the white stallion would stay close by. White dove lit a kerosene lantern from the covered wagon and held it in position for hungry to see. He moved fast while unloading the Gatling gun from the carriage and sliding it off the backboards down the wooden beams. He also emptied it of all other supplies he had collected and then pushed the entire empty carriage down the vertical shaft. Hungry remembered several other items he had thrown down the shaft before; some were gunfighters he had crossed paths with. By now, their skeletons would have been picked clean by maggots and whatever other creatures lived in the darkness way down deep.

He had hidden the entrance of the cave by molding dirt, clay, and rocks into a wall and then planting ferns and grasses in between the exposed bigger rocks. The blocked entrance looked natural, with the landscape coming into the tunnel where the first vertical shaft jogged your attention away from it. After a few hours of working, he had opened up a hole big enough to squeeze it through. After he got inside the hole, the cave opened, and he lit some of his candles. A little farther in the back was where he kept a lot of his treasure: all of his bigger stuff like the inventor's gadgets, his electrical generating boxes, and medical supplies. Hungry returned to the narrow opening and proceeded to make it wider.

He tied ropes onto the Gatling gun and dragged it into the opening. It barely fit through the entrance. Hungry had wrapped it with animal skins and burlap to keep it from picking up dirt and make it easier to slide. It was an awesome thing to look at: polished brass, copper, and gleaming metal. He played the scene through his mind of it ripping apart the army man and law man that had almost buried them alive. It blew them into pieces. He was lucky they left the white stallion at camp because almost all of their other horses were massacred. He made a foundation out of some railroad ties and secured the Gatling gun to it with ropes. There was a spot where the cave was chiseled through straight rock for about 20 feet after the entrance, and he figured if he had to fire this thing, that would be the safest place without a cave-in. He pointed it so it was aiming at the entrance and laid all the bullet bands on a shelf for easy loading. The crank arm spun around, loading bullets into rotating barrels that fired them as fast as you could turn the handle. It was truly a piece of awesome machinery. He remembered reading that the Gatling gun was designed by the American inventor Dr. Richard J Gatling, and it was patented on November 4, 1862. Gatling wrote that he created it to reduce the number of deaths by combat and disease and to stop the war. The US Army adopted Gatling guns in several calibers, including .42, .45, .50, .70 and 1-inch calibers.

Chapter 8

Returning To The Cavern

After moving some large flat stones and earth and crawling inside the cave, they started lighting all the candles and cranking the handle of the electrical generator box. The 'FireWire' jar lights began to flicker to life. Hungry opened a bottle out of a crate of Baker's Pure Rye Whiskey. They each took a drink and started to work their way through some of the back tunnels, crawling over fallen rocks and debris while following a vein of quarts that ran horizontally in the cave. The whiskey burned their throats and made their eyes water as they moved.

After a good amount of exertion and squeezing through narrow passageways, they reached an opening wider than a chuck wagon. This was where a lot of the gold and jewels Hungry had acquired aligned the walls, covered with burlap and hides. There were carved ledges made of dried clay and granite stone on one wall. On the other wall, there were stacks of crates—all the way up to the ceiling, row by row, seemingly holding back the stone-cut passageway.

Golden clocks and candleholders of silver, gold, and stone held candles that they lit to light up the corridor. Shiny decanters encrusted with diamonds, chalices, and jeweled swords were revealed after removing more burlap. There was an ancient shining Viking crown of white gold with long shark-tooth-shaped raw diamonds, jagged rubies, and smaller emeralds the size of oak egg corns. The sparse light reflected off of the jeweled surface of the white metal band.

Hungry had robbed most of the loot from the antique museum train cars headed to Sacramento and San Francisco. They were all laid out, sparkling along the shelves with many other oversized gemstone necklaces and pieces of jewelry. Hungry liked to uncover it all and stare at its shimmer. It reflected candlelight and electricity together. It gave him energy—almost like the Crystal Water. He dressed White Dove in the most beautiful diamond and ruby necklaces and rainbow-colored gemstone rings and bracelets. He told her they were hers to keep forever.

Farther to the back of the cavern, around a couple of corners, grew many huge multicolored crystals. They were made of quartz and other minerals. Some shined with colors beyond this world, radiating their own light and softly, quietly humming, like they were giving off some kind of musical frequency. Hungry knew his stones and jewelry well, and he kept some of his highest quality gems and jewels here, but he had never seen anything like these crystals, nor had he shared them with anyone. They had been his secret alone… until now.

He was opening a long, slender, oak steamer box where

he kept his finest guns, belts, and boots. He changed into some armadillo he had. They were gray with black soles. He had taken them from a Mexican bandit during a shoot-out when he was robbing a Wells Fargo carriage for the gold box. Hungry had ended up with it and many more—he had collected several of the Wells Fargo boxes full of gold, some he had never even opened. He was labeled a notorious train bandit and stagecoach robber at a young age.

In his later teenage years, he would rob the gold shipments, leaving the Lincoln Train Station. Using kerosene, he would light fires that blocked the train cars' aisles and exit and entry points. Then, he would count all of the guards, and when their attention was on the fires, he would open gunfire. He would shoot with both hands until he killed every one of them, always saving the train conductor for last, making him stop somewhere he could easily unload all the gold.

There were several boxes in this cave, buried closer to the front but well-hidden. Beyond them was where the now huge crystals grew—neon blue and green, growing upward and downward off the walls like giant dinosaur teeth, jagged and sharp. Larger mineral deposits of tanzanite, tourmaline, and amethyst also lined the floors and ceilings. They seemed to have grown huge since they first entered the cave. In an upward tunnel they could see above them, giant purple and green shards grew, fluorescent and bright greenish yellow.

Sparkling water trickled from little springs in the wall and then swirled and pooled up before it turned to steam again, condensing on another crystal surface to drip the color of rainbows. The mist cloud of water made you think you were standing inside a rainbow. They breathed in the mist; the vapors smelled of damp earth and minerals and were sweet like candy.

Hungry had explored the cave as a young teenager, and that was the first time he tasted it. They drank from the swirling pool, and they both felt it tingle inside their bodies. Almost instantly, Hungry felt rejuvenated. All of his senses were heightened, and his hair started standing on end. They looked at each other and laughed. They both got goosebumps on their necks and arms.

Hungry motioned for White Dove to have more of it. She liked the sweet taste. He was sure it was not poisonous since it had never harmed him, and it did not have a bitter taste in the slightest. She sipped from a golden chalice he had filled with the crystal water. It had an electric color and vapor coming from it. It was sweet, so they added whiskey to it.

After a while, they returned to the shelved cavern room and opened another crate. This one had miniature steam engines, magnetic perpetual motors, and golden clocks with glass windows, allowing you to see the silver gears and turning mechanisms, and there were other tiny machines capable of producing electrical current. Most of them were forged of some sort of precious metal. They marveled at some of the intricate designs and the imaginative genius that the inventors of these mechanisms had as they looked at the turning metal parts. Their eyes grew wide and sparkled, their minds meshed even closer together, and their heartbeats grew louder.

Suddenly, they heard the faint sound of horse hooves striking stone. Hungry had not sealed up the side entrance to the cave, and the sound reverberated back to them. They also heard the white stallion snorting. They sat down there and listened curiously and then with lightning-quick reflexes, gathered their guns and headed for the entrance of the cave.

The outside air was cool. There was a sliver of a moon and a few stars. From the sound of it, riders were approaching them fast. There were at least half a dozen of them. The trail split right before their cave entrance, and their white stallion had actually jumped into the upper cave tunnel. It had somehow made it to a ledge and was looking down at Hungry like it was time to ride or die.

Hungry had a whole array of guns he had laid out, freshly oiled and loaded. He took them out and placed them in hidden areas along the trail to the cave. The first rider skidded to a halt if as his horse sensed the coming gun volley, and it bucked its rider into the horse behind him.

That was when Hungry appeared, guns blazing, rapidly firing from the hip, dealing them a wrath of his 40. Caliber death delivered swiftly. Six of the surviving government men from the cattle town of Penryn were here for the Gatling gun. They were now all dead. Mr. Valencia was pierced through the throat with one of White Dove's arrows. He was the last man to speak. When he looked at Hungry, blood was gurgling from his throat and mouth, and he whispered something incomprehensible with his last breath. Was it "Bitch?" Hungry winked at him, smiling wide, showing his diamond and ruby teeth fillings. Moonlight reflected off the jewels and the green in his eyes.

Hungry and White Dove gathered all of the guns and gold once again. None of them had any boots or hats worthy of saving. They tied their bodies to their horses and drove them back down the canyon, far away from the caves and the trails that led to their entrance. The gang of lawmen had ridden fast and furious right to their deaths.

Hungry was eating their food; it was the same steak he'd had in the bar that night. He took time to clear the trail of all signs of the shootout. They stayed close along the river's edge for a few hours, resting in the nooks of moss-covered rocks and long grass. They lay in each other's arms while waiting for more ambushers or lawmen to arrive. The moon rose higher in the sky, its velvety black canopy pierced by the glimmer of stars. Crickets sounded off, and there was the hoot of the white owl that seemed to follow them.

When completely satisfied, they waited even longer for signs of more travelers or any sound of intruders. They explored and comforted each other as they drank a mixture of crystal water from the cave and Baker's Pure Rye Whiskey from their canteens. They had acquired even more high-end bourbon whiskey from the horseman. They headed back to the cave to seal the entrance and wipe away any other signs of tracks leading to it. They gathered some of the stuff they wanted and hid away some of the treasure they had unboxed.

It was morning by the time they left the cave once again, covering their tracks this time as well. They were both on horseback. The white stallion had perched on the ledge of the upper cave shaft and was waiting for them. They were not even tired, though they should have been; the cave water kept them alert and awake in a strong, black coffee sort of way.

They ate more beef jerky and drank more whiskey and water as they continued hiding their trails for miles. The sunrise was radiant, a golden sphere of fire spearing—shafts of light shining into their eyes and off their buckles, jewelry, shiny metal guns, and bandoleros. They focused ahead. The stallion wanted to speed up and gallop, so they raced on through the afternoon, stopping to hunt and eat a deer or whatever animals they rode upon. White Dove could shoot an arrow through a running rabbit from 200 feet. They shot and ate deer, rabbit, squirrel, pheasant, and quail.

They traveled west, back toward the town of Lincoln, through the valley's meadows to the mountain trails. The air smelled fresh, like pine needles and wildflower petals. There was now another sunset, this time violent red, with purple hues and slivers of yellow. The sun was setting behind the mountain range that looked prehistoric. Hungry thought of the sabretooth tiger skull he had hidden in one of the caves. He also had dinosaur bones—yes, he collected everything, but this view of the sunset, with White Dove next to him, was truly something to marvel at.

From the top of the mountains, they could see small groups of fire that could have been torches or campfires. Either way, it meant there were many individuals. They took their horse back to a clearing, and he knew to wait for them. White Dove was sharpening arrows, wrapping them in bundles of six or eight. She was also prepping her perfume bottle flint.

They took shelter behind a giant rock with a downed log. It made a perfect bench for them to prepare for what was to come. It was hours later before they had quietly crawled close enough to actually see what was going on.

Flickering torchlight shined off pale white faces covered in war paint and tattoos: bones, teeth, and shells inlaid in their skin with fragments of stones. The whites of their eyes seemed deadened to their mutilations. They had chest plates of bone and metals, spears, and knives with huge obsidian or metal blades. There were at least a dozen of them, holding torches and shrilling in high-pitched screams at the full moon in the night sky. A huge campfire ring of stone with giant logs perched over it cooked chunks of bloody meat in a giant metal cauldron. There was a slender older female, the troglodyte priestess or queen, setting naked on a throne made of bones and skulls. She was perched on the rocky cliff outcropping. She was painted or covered in powder that was pure white.

A huge, bloodstained disk held one of the government gunmen—it was Mr. Valencia. They had stripped him and rubbed him in salt, molasses, and herbs. He was roasting like a Sunday hog: freshly bludgeoned, gutted, and seasoned. Hungry thought to himself that he really smelled like bacon.

More cave dwellers appeared. They, too, had pearl-white skin. Their faces and necks were tattooed and adorned with ivory, animal bones, and teeth implants. Their ear lobes and faces were pierced and torn, and their eyes looked like windows into death.

The sky was dark as oil, and the wind was still and silent. They were preparing another giant, shiny, metal platter of meat and roots. The light from their torches and firelight reflected off their bodies. Their shrill chanting grew louder until the high priestess made her entrance.

Wide eyes rolled back into her head, whites shining only—no pupil, no iris. Pierced flesh with horns and antlers through her breasts and shells and bones hanging from her ears, cheeks, and neck. She stood tall, skeletal, strangely tattooed, and mostly naked. Steam rose off her body.

Hungry could see several cave entrances along the pathway of these cave dwellers. White Dove sat in disbelief. She remembered hearing the tale as a little girl from her mother about her father's grandmother, who was one of the cave dweller Indians, living underground like bugs until they came out to feast. They would stay sedated with some herbal root while they hibernated. They mutilated their partially naked bodies and communicated in strange, high-pitched animal sounds. They captured and ate humans for ritual pleasure, lived in the darkest caves deep underground, and only came out once every full moon to feast on humans.

White Dove was uncomfortable here and did not want to kill them, either. She knew that Hungry could. She knew he had sensed her uneasiness and had also realized there were more of them hidden than they could see—possibly hundreds. They watched the ceremony for a little longer in suspense as the tribe men and women gathered in increasingly large numbers to the feast. The underdwellers smoked long-feathered bone pipes, ate fungi, and drank mixtures of rotten manure and blood as they mated and shrieked like crazed animals toward the stars.

Mr. Valencia's carcass was completely picked clean. Only his ivory white skeleton bones remained. They even ate his brains and eyeballs. Hungry had watched long enough and motioned for White Dove to go back up the trail silently. They would get far away from there... fast. It made them both feel uneasy. They returned to their horse and started a fast trot toward Lincoln. They could still hear the shrieking screams of the troglodytes as they looked to the skies. The horse broke into a fast gallop, following the Washington trail in the waning autumn moonlight.

Hours passed, and they stopped to water the horse. They came to a ravine that Hungry knew very well. It came from the town of Auburn. He had a couple of cave hideouts along its route and was in the mood to lay down for the night. It would be morning soon, and he needed a couple of hours of shut-eye to stay clearheaded, sharp, and focused.

They came to a sandy embankment next to the ravine and decided to make a campfire. They shot a deer, cleaned it, and roasted it on the campfire. They sipped on whiskey and smoked tobacco. Completely well-versed in their own language by now, they talked, and Hungry explained that this was the town where he grew up. Somewhere in there, his mother and father could be alive, but he had not seen them in many, many years, nor did he care to.

Now, however, he had less hatred for his mother. Was she still alive, or did she come to a violent end like a lot of the whores he'd known as a child? He explained how he had given her a bag of gold the last time he had seen her, but afterward, he thought it might have been the wrong move. He was hoping she did not overdose on alcohol or medicines or get robbed or killed for it. He would be embarrassed if they found her, but he was used to it.

Chapter 9

The Gates Of Hell

They ate their roasted deer meat and tethered the white stallion close by, then closed their eyes and slept for the remainder of the night. They awoke to the sounds of foreign language. They could hear voices of walking men talking back-and-forth in an Asian dialect. Some of it soft and hurried, while other louder men yelled for them to shut their mouths and be quiet.

They were getting close to Hungry and Dove, so the two crossed the ravine and spied on the column of walking men from a distance camouflaged in the bushes. They were on the trail that ran downhill to the giant vertical shaft cave. They called them the gates of hell because some of the caves down the shafts went so far that no one who had been to their end was now alive.

After watching them from a closer distance, Hungry and Dove realized they were workers or miners. Maybe they were going to dig a tunnel. The railroad was about ten miles in the other direction, so Hungry was a little curious. Most likely, they were going to make a tunnel somewhere. The Chinese were responsible for building much of the railroad tracks, and they did all the blasting through hills, mountains, and rocks to make passageways for the Southern Pacific railroad.

The riders on horseback seemed to be an unruly bunch, hurrying along the walking Chinese men. The ones on foot motioned that they wanted a break and kept saying "rest," but the riders kept forcing them forward, so they walked along in silence. There must've been at least a hundred of them all together, including the men on horseback.

Hungry recognized them as the railroad men. They were well-armed, and they usually had gold in their saddlebags. After following for hours, the men finally halted the column and took a break. Hungry noticed that the Chinese had their own food, wore clothes that hung loosely, and had pointy hats. Only a few of them had swords; most of them carried shovels, picks, and other digging implements.

They made a quick camp and started cooking food. Hungry noticed the way the men on horseback watched the few men that had swords. They were samurai swords; Hungry realized he had a few hidden in his caves. They were forged of domestic steel, folded over and over in burning red hot coals. The sword metal was crafted by masters of ironwork. Hungry recognized that a few of the sword men looked as if they were descendants of the samurai.

Hungry and White Dove settled in their own camp after watching for a couple of hours. They back-tracked and found higher ground. They walked along the ridge line and kept an eye on the encampment.

This particular mountain range had many cave entrances, with giant granite and quartz rocks the size of chuck wagons. Gold veins were not uncommon to find in the caves—crystallized gold in its rawest form was a treat to look at. Sometimes, its surfaces shone with shades of metallic purples, greens, and blues. Hungry had some crystals of gold that were the size of shotgun shells, and they were trophy pieces that he robbed from the gold museums in Sacramento. It was a shame that there were still so many people sucking up all the gold of the land, he thought.

They were about to leave; they had grown tired of watching the railroad crew. Hungry still didn't understand what they were doing this far out. They gathered their stuff and headed west again. He was hoping the government was not going to build a railroad right along the route, where all of his caves were that hid his loot.

After less than a mile of traveling, they came upon a burning wagon train with four or five wagons in a circle. Half of them were charcoaled, and the other ones were still smoldering—you could see arrows stuck in the sides of the coaches and a few slumped bodies that now resembled pincushions. They concluded that Indians had raided them, and they were not far from here.

Hungry and Dove back-tracked again just in time to hear

gunfire erupt from the railroad encampment. There was shouting and screaming, different dialects yelling frantically. The men were being corralled by the horsemen and forced to follow the trail. Hungry and Dove followed them in silence.

After a few miles, they came to several cave entrances. They kept going down a trail that wound around corners and over rocky ledges until they came to the Gates of Hell. Hungry and Dove watched as the horsemen forced the walking Chinese men into the cave. They were telling them to take their shovels and dig a tunnel.

However, as the men entered the cave, the horsemen open-fired and forced the remaining men to run into the cave into darkness. The men who were running away did not realize there were downshafts. There was no way for their rifles to miss them as they were running through the darkness and falling to their deaths. Hungry and Dove watched all the gunmen circling the entrance, shooting the Chinese workers and forcing them into the cave.

Hungry and Dove started shooting the men on horseback; their backs were to them, and they did not see it coming. They blasted the backs of their heads with 12 gauge buckshot shotgun loads. The led ripped most of their skulls completely apart. They sat still; their cowboy boots were stuck in their stirrups, as their bodies slumped forward on their horses for a few seconds as if they had not realized they were dead.

It happened so fast that the remaining Chinese workers had not realized they were safe yet. Their eyes were wide open and white against the red on their faces. They were all splattered with the blood, brains, and skull pieces of the railroad horsemen.

Hungry remembered he had heard tales of the railroad men hiring groups of workers to dig tunnels, and then before they paid them, they would leave them in a caved-in tunnel. The railroad men were ruthless—they would steal the land of the weak, kill the strong, and would forcibly take the land of anyone in their path if they didn't sell it cheap. There was no way to stop the United States Railroad.

The smoke from the gunfire settled, and the remaining men regained their senses. There was one man still alive with a sword, and he was taking charge. They looked at Hungry and White Dove as they wiped their faces and looked at their hands—they were all calloused and bruised and swollen. One man with a samurai sword turned to Hungry and bowed, and the rest of them followed suit immediately, all bowing and conveying their deepest gratitude with the look in their eyes.

Hungry walked to the dead railroad men who were still slumped over their horses and emptied their saddlebags. He threw the gold and the weapons to the samurai men. They did, however, find several bottles of Old Tub Jim Beam bourbon whiskey that he had kept a few of. The horsemen had fancy guns and boots, but Hungry did not want any of them. He left them all to the Chinese men, and he and Dove retreated into the darkness.

They took their cliffside trail back up to the top of the mountain range, where the white stallion awaited them. By the time they got to the top of the mountain line, where they could see the lights of the Lincoln train station, Hungry and Dove were a little tipsy from the Beam whiskey.

They found a grassy plateau among the oak trees and mossy rocks. They were protected by cliffs, and they rolled out their makeshift sleeping mat of animal skins, furs, and hides. They did not have to worry about the Indians that had raided the wagon train party, and they were not worried about the Chinese tunnel workers since they had saved half of them. Maybe they would run into the Indians with their new rifles and slaughter each other before they woke up, Hungry figured. He would hear them if they came close—he had his horse on the lookout, and his senses were heightened, as were White Dove's. He could move as fast as lightning, and his mind was always on high alert for any movement or sound of intruders. They fell asleep laying on their backs, resting their heads on a saddle, holding each other, watching the sun creep over the horizon. They woke up after many hours. Leaves were rustling in the trees, and then they heard the song of birds, chattering and chirping. The sun had risen in the ocean blue sky to indicate that it was mid-morning; the smell of pine and damp earth stirred their senses.

Chapter 10

The Trail to Lincoln

Large birds terrified White Dove. She still had nightmares of buzzards eating her alive. She clung on to Hungry; she had explained to him what happened to her eyelid, and the scars on her body were a reminder. Hungry held her and shook his head, telling her that she no longer had to fear anything. They were the ultimate hunters, and every animal and man in nature was their prey.

He realized her hatred was more intense than her fear. He had to get over hating dogs. He shook his head as he drew his pistols and dropped every bird in the tree. They fell like clay pigeons at the shooting gallery from the circus in town. Feathers floated in the air, and a mild breeze took them away. It was silent, and they took in the moment, knowing that they had to get active in case someone heard his gunshots.

He did not care. He anticipated the engagement. He knew he was not unstoppable, and that humbleness made him even more deadly in gun battles. They saddled up the white stallion, broke camp, and, eating jerked rabbit meat, trotted down the trail toward Lincoln. No other travelers seemed to be in the area as they rode.

Behind them, not far away, something followed their

trail, staying far enough away not to be sensed, heard, or seen—another lone predator, watching and learning, and it was also always hungry.

They were coming out of the cover of the mountains and tree line into a meadow of flowing long, green grass. Huge growths of green brush and star thistle pooled. In certain areas, the tops of some of the plants were six feet tall and sharp enough to poke your eye out.

This area housed the dreadful poison oak bushes that, if you didn't know about them, would leave you in a violently itchy rash from head to toe if you itched it enough. Hungry had a sample of its poison once; it had made his face swell up, his eyelids had looked inflated, and he was in an itchy frenzy, nearly scratching all his skin off. No one had ever told him not to touch it—he had learned most things he knew the hard way.

Along the trail, there were other poisonous bushes and animals. Of all of them, the rattlesnake was the worst. Hungry had seen men with necks bitten by a rattlesnake— swollen with bruised skin leaking pus out of the bite marks. He knew some died if they didn't cut an X into the bite marks and suck out the venom.

They followed the widening trail into a flatland bordered by water-cut ditches ten and twenty feet deep. Some had water in the basin. The sky was clear, and the mild breeze carried a scent of dogwood flowers and pine. There was no sign of riders in any direction, so they stopped at a place where the water pooled in granite slabs of rock. Ferns and other evergreen foliage grew from the rocks and moist pockets of dirt. They let the stallion water while they prepared to hunt. They had seen deer and rabbits along the trail that they could sneak back without the horse to shoot.

Hunting with a partner was way quicker, and it had its advantages. Hungry would go up the ditch lines while White Dove would sit across from the trail, perched on a rock with a quiver of arrows ready. Hungry would flush the animals towards her as she shot them silently and seemingly effortlessly, never wasting an arrow or missing a shot. The animals would drop, silent and still, as she shot more and more of them. After a few deer and several rabbits were downed, Dove whistled for Hungry to come in.

More animals still came, but she had enough for a few days, so she watched them run past. She caught a brief glimpse of an animal's head through a thicket of cattails. It was big and had huge fangs or canines of some kind, she thought. It was so fast that she had doubts initially, but then she realized it was real. It was quiet for a few minutes. Then, when Hungry returned, they gathered the animals, and she pointed to where she had seen the animal. She told him about how fast and big it was. Hungry checked his bullets and started dragging all the bodies of the rabbits and deer over by the cattails. He cleaned them there and left a pile of guts for whatever his White Dove had seen.

They headed back to where the giant, green-leaved plants and ferns were growing off the rocks by the pool of water. They also kept a lookout for a bear—it was close, they knew. They had seen its tracks by the water earlier; still, they bathed, lit campfires, and laid out naked on the granite slabs.

Later, they laid out some of the cut-up portions of meat they salted to be dried by the sun and fire-heated rocks. Hungry oiled their guns and checked their ammo belts. White Dove washed their clothes and apparel, smoked tobacco, and sipped from a bottle of Beam whiskey they had in the saddle bags. Together they watched the sun move to the west and prepared for the darkness of the first hours of the night.

Hungry made himself comfortable and watched as the sky's colors changed into darker shades as the twilight diminished. White Dove moved on to drinking moonshine, pure white lightning from a teacup while she sat on a tree stump by the campfire. The last thing they noticed as the sun went down was its reflection off some barbed wire strung on fence posts further along the trail they would be going down. They kept the white stallion close to them as it grew dark.

Ever since Hungry and Dove had last drank the sweet Crystal water, they only needed a few hours of sleep per night. They woke up at around midnight when the moon was shining bright. The campfire was just red coals now, and the meat was all dried, cooked well enough for travel. They packed their supplies and started to leave camp. The moon's light lit the trail enough to see the route ahead as the silhouettes of six horsemen riding toward them appeared. The two drew closer to the six.

Hungry let White Dove talk to them—she had practiced using words and could now make sentences. They came close and stopped about twenty feet away. "We don't want trouble," she said. "My husband is wounded. We are going to Lincoln to get help." They were both ready to shoot if the men had any bad intentions, but they wanted to play it out and see what the gang wanted and who they were. The riders approached closer and pulled up about three feet away. They were obviously not going to be polite. The horsemen in the front had rifles in their hands resting on their saddle pommel. Hungry kept his face hidden so they wouldn't see the gleam of the jewels in his mouth. He had made a pretty good name for himself, and word of his gun-fighting abilities had spread like wildfire.

White Dove asked them what they wanted, and the leader replied, "We will take your booty and whatever is in those saddlebags."

The lead rider smiled wickedly. He was a short, curly-haired man with a long mustache, wearing dirty clothes and a black leather hat. It was decorated with turquoise stones and silver beads wrapped around its band.

She looked at them, spat, and said, "Okay, have me then." Hungry drew out his two .45 caliber six guns simultaneously and blew pieces of their chests out of their backs. He then quickly shot the other riders. Hungry could hear the air, sucked into their lungs through their mouth, escape as it exited out of the bullet holes. Their guns didn't even get a chance to fire; their mouths brought them instant death. They had breathed it in with their last words.

They slumped forward in their saddles and slowly slid off their mounts. Their slack bodies thumped on the ground like sacks of grain. Their horses just stood there. There were six of them, and each of them had taken two bullets in the chest.

Hungry's pistols were empty, so he reloaded as he whistled his favorite Sunday church hymn. White Dove looked at him, curious and in awe—he was so fast to the draw. She picked up the leader's hat with the turquoise stones, brushed it off, and put it in her saddle bag. They looked at each other and smiled. The extra horses were prime, but they were comfortable riding together on the white stallion; it was easier to hide one horse's tracks, and the stallion actually knew how to hide itself too.

Hungry and White Dove looked over all the bodies and emptied their pockets. They weren't railroad men or cattle ranchers—they were all kind of sour-smelling, like all the other heathens that preyed on wayward travelers and pioneer families. Hungry shots some rounds off in the air close to the horses in order to scare them off. They all ran back down the trail they came from. The men had some gold coins and decent guns. Hungry piled their bodies off the trail, poured kerosene on them, and lit them on fire. They stood upwind and watched them burn for a few minutes until the meat on their faces started hissing, sizzling, and popping. They looked at each other and winced. Hungry and White Dove gathered the gold, guns, and knives and mounted the white stallion, which didn't hesitate to get the hell out of there, galloping fast, heading towards the town of Lincoln.

It was about 2 A.M., and the stars were bright in a sky painted of dark blues with black and white brush strokes. Following the trail in stealth was the creature White Dove had seen by the cattails. It had devoured all of the bones and intestines left for it and was curiously following them. She had told Hungry her first name was Alita, but she preferred when Hungry called her his White Dove. They galloped on until the sunrise appeared, cutting with razors of golden light sabers through the morning sky.

"This is the trail," Hungry thought out loud. They had travelled for a few hours and then took a smaller pathway off the main trail that led to some of his hideouts. He often traveled and checked to see that his cave entrances were still hidden and undisturbed. He had made so many false walls; he learned how to make them stick even through the hardest rains. Some caves could not be closed up—their entrances had to be set in just the right area of a hillside or cliff. There were many that he left undisturbed so that miners or fellow travelers could use them overnight when needed without finding his hideouts.

They were only a half day's ride away from Lincoln now; they would be pulling up before dark, he figured. It had been at least seven years since Hungry had been back home. When he was young, he wondered about the place so many times. Would there be wanted adds still hanging throughout the town with his picture and a reward offered? He thought of his mother…(was she still alive?) or his father, and if he was still alive. He had tried to stop giving either of them a thought, but now again, he wondered if they had met their end yet, if they got a proper burial, or if their carcasses were just left somewhere on the plains for coyotes and buzzards to eat? He pondered that question quite often to himself.

As they traveled along the trail, he noticed a few more cabins off on hillsides and in some of the valleys and meadows. They passed a gold miner who had a horse and a carriage, and his wife was riding shotgun. His horses were small and skinny, but there was no feeling that they were bad people. In his younger years, he would have murdered them because the people looked well-fed and clean-cut, but now, he wasn't quite as mean, and he could read a man when they looked him in the eye, and the fellow on the wagon seemed genuine. He was not afraid to look Hungry in the eye and showed no sign of being intolerant or prejudiced. They passed each other on the trail without any issues.

Hungry was a little excited. He was getting closer to the place where he had grown up. Yes, he had killed a lot of people in the town, and the train station massacre was his most infamous, but he knew different people always came and went into that town. He left at an early age—no heartache, no heartbreak. He knew he was born into a world full of pain, and it would devour him if he didn't resist it. He soon would find out if anyone would recognize him.

He would always keep going on and never give up—certainly not now that he had a different life with his White Dove. He knew he was quick-minded and strong enough to kill anything that got in his way. He was like a lightning bolt, appearing in an instant, flashy and deadly to everything. He had stood up one time in church and said before being kicked out, "Hell yeah, listen up all you sinning sons of bitches, if you're not truly righteous, I will kill you and take your gold, and if you are evil or mean to women and children, I will find you and kill you and take your soul and your gold and light you on fire, you sinning sons of bitches. You can never hide from the wrath of Hungry Jack Hollow, for I will strike you as quick as lightning, amen". He was asked by the preacher to never return.

Nightfall was about over and a tang of the morning sunlight squinted on the horizon as they pulled into the town of Lincoln. It was not completely dark at the train station. Was it still a major transport for all of the gold that was prospected? Did all the gold still stockpile in the town bank before it left the depo? Many miners and prospectors still traded in their gold for coins or cash dollars, and the Wells Fargo wagons still collected gold and left the station to Sacramento, San Francisco, or who knows where, but a lot of the gold was mined up. Some said aliens were involved in collecting all the gold, but Jack no longer cared; he had a hell of a lot of treasure and gold buried between here and El Dorado.

Hungry remembered when he was really young, on that mountainside, when he saw the giant for the first time. It seemed like a lifetime ago when he had enjoyed the company of the giant magnificent beast, knowing that he was so rare and thought to be so dangerous. He was feeling melancholy, knowing he had probably seen the last of them. There were no more giants known to live in the mountains of California, most likely because all of the people killed them. Their skeletons remained in a couple of museums. Hungry knew that some grew to be over 26 feet tall. He had seen them walking through the mountains, breaking treetops, and causing rockslides that would take out trails. They were not of this earth, he thought, as he walked along, watching the burning kerosene lights of the town grow closer and brighter.

The sheriff's station was a dimly lit building next to the courthouse. Several townspeople were walking along the streets and boardwalk, and there were carriages and horses on the streets. The sound of the steam engine pulling into the train station—brakes squeaking, horn bellowing, the earth rumbling from the vibration of the rails—it all brought back a nostalgic memory.

They watched the skyline become slightly more illuminated as the sun approached its horizon in the eastern mountains. A wildly colorful wagon cart, drawn by two donkeys, approached them. The writing on the cart proclaimed tinctures from the fountains of youth, elixirs that stopped the sands of time, and medicines that kept you feeling young and strong forever, promising eternal wisdom and infinite health. The driver was an old, wrinkly, hunched-back shell of a man. He had a suit on that was dusty and stained from the roads he had traveled on. Hungry noticed he seemed very drunk, and his hat was too big for his head.

They passed the saloon and brothel where he had been fostered in his youth. The town had changed a little—it seemed like it had gotten smaller. The wood-fronted buildings, hotels, and church seemed fresh and newly-oiled. They pulled into the stable behind the hotel, took off their saddlebags, and flipped a silver dollar to the stable boy. Jack told him to take good care of the stallion and that he would give him a gold coin in the morning.

The stable boy looked at Hungry in awe: his shiny pearl-handle Colt .45 caliber pistols, his jeweled teeth gleaming on his face, rattlesnake boots, and Stetson hat. His girl was something to look at, too, with her slender build, white hair, and milky complexion. She had nice curves under her white garments and hides, and she always seemed to look radiant and attractive. She changed her eyelash color often; they were usually the only part of her with color. That night, she had somehow made them long and blue. They hid the damage from the vultures that had attacked her, and her scar gave her character just as Hungry's did.

They took their saddlebags to the hotel desk clerk and had him check them into a safe. They paid for a room but headed for the saloon. A couple of passer-byers stared in disbelief. Kids dashed through the alleyways and backstreets, yelling and pretending to have gunfights. There were a couple of number ones. He always kept count of the potential threats or hostile cowboys.

The gas streetlamps burning along Main Street cast shadows on faces and distorted them as they strolled along the walking boards. Hungry looked down through the cracks, remembering the passageways and hidden corridors he had made as a child.

They heard laughter and many voices as they approached the saloon doors. This town was alive all night. Usually, the town didn't shut down until one or two in the afternoon, and then only for a few hours of sleep due to the gamblers, gunfighters, gold prospectors, and train stations's schedule. Lights from the inside shined off the colored liquor bottles on the shelves behind the bar. There were probably 14 or 15 people besides the barkeep. They went to the first barstools on the counter, the same place Hungry had bought his first drink many years ago. He ordered whiskey sours for both of them. No one seemed to pay them any mind, although the talking had grown quieter.

Several men were gambling around a table, smoking tobacco, and carrying on. They looked at each other and breathed in the air. Hungry rolled some smokes, and they tipped the piano man to start playing something. They paid with silver dollars so as not to draw attention to themselves. They had stuffed their pockets with gold coins, and they were packing some guns and ammo. Not one soul looked familiar to Hungry. He took in everyone and rated them; no one seemed to want to start a fight. That was different and unusual for Hungry.

He had a different air about him now, too. He bathed more now and smelt good, too—White Dove had fragrance oils and soaps that she made from wildflowers, honey, and animal tallow. They were enjoying the lighting and the whiskey. A couple of dancing girls mingled with them. Hungry bought them drinks. A drifter leaning against the wall by the door was keeping an eye on them, but he was no threat to Hungry. They asked if food was available and ordered several steaks to go. They drank whiskey sours, smoked rolled tobacco, and listened to the piano player.

Chapter 11

Candy Corns And Rhinestone Studded Holsters

Hungry started practicing drawing fast at a young age. He used the smaller 22-cal pistols to practice double draws firing off the hip. He was tall and skinny from a young age and knew how to lean into the recoil to keep his shots straight. It took lighting quick reflexes to be a gunfighter, and you had to have superior hand-to-eye coordination to not be shot by your opponent. Most gunfighters died tragically young. You also had to be calm and level-headed during a gunfight and not be too anxious to shoot before aiming.

When Hungry was five, he would practice twirling his six-shooters, holstering them and unholstering them as fast as he could while chewing bubblegum or eating corn candies. He always had his pocketknives and switchblades in his boots and pockets, but holsters were more a part of him than his pants. His love for guns had never let him down.

Hungry and Dove stood close to one another as more people came into the saloon. The piano player was wearing a wrinkled shirt and stained hat. Lying on the piano was a thin, curly-haired, burlesque girl. She was singing a ballad about a gal who was a wild horse-taming gunfighter. There was a strong smell of burnt tobacco and distilled whiskey in the air. Lights burned red with flames flickering from kerosene-drenched-wicks. Lavender-scented candle wax and tobacco smoke filled the air. It was also thick with laughter and badgering voices.

Hungry ate many plates of steaks and paid the barkeep in gold coins. He thought to himself that the saloon owner looked a little familiar, but the bartender did not. He decided he would have a look around and see what was going on throughout the building. When Hungry went to the back of the saloon to see who else was around, he saw several men gathering and grouping up at the sheriff's station. He slid between the buildings quietly and watched for a spell to see what all the commotion was about.

Sure enough, the leaning man from the bar was at the sheriff's station, pointing towards the bar, talking to the sheriff and all his men. Hungry knew he had to get back to the bar fast and get White Dove out. On his way back inside, he noticed a few gallons of kerosene stacked next to the rear stable of the saloon. He gathered them, covered them with a horse blanket, and carried them back to the rear of the bar. He left them right outside the back door exit and went inside.

White Dove was at the bar. A few people were around her, but none seemed to be threatening. They were asking her what her name was and where she came from. They seemed to be polite. She knew a little English by now, so she told them her name was Alita. One of the Englishmen said to her, "that means 'wings,'" and then she said that her friends called her 'White Dove.' As she said it, she realized that Hungry was her only friend. She gazed down at her rhinestone-studded holsters and ammo belt housing her .38 caliber death. White Dove thought to herself, "These fine people sure treated her nicely."

Hungry approached and nodded to them, keeping his jeweled teeth side of the face hidden. They drank their drinks and nodded to the barman. He made a gesture for them to go out the back, saying that the sheriff was coming for them. Hungry appreciated his honesty, and they left swiftly out the back entrance just as the sheriff and his men were coming in through the front door of the saloon.

Hungry and White Dove grabbed the kerosene containers and headed to the sheriff's station. It was abandoned except for a molester who was in the lock-up— the iron cage had a chalkboard above its door and had labeled him. A couple of gallons of kerosene were just enough to cover the entire floor of the jailhouse. They poured the last of it on their way out the door and lit it on fire.

The flame started out small—blue and green—but quickly grew into an inferno of red and orange flames. The molester screamed and shouted; he was about to see what

Hell looked like. The crackling and popping of the fire overlapped his last futile attempts to scream. They watched him hanging onto the bars, squirming like he was being electrocuted until the flames were all they could see.

The heat was so intense they had to back away. They went down the alleyway into the shadows. They could see the street lighting up just as the sheriff's men came from the front and the back of the saloon. There, they all stood and looked at the burning jail. Half of them looked dumbfounded, while some stomped their feet, and the others began looking for the two of them.

In that instant, Hungry and Dove open-fired, Hungry taking the men on the left and White Dove on the right. There was a group of at least a dozen men that just took in the bullets. A couple of them just cleared leather with their weapons before being blasted in the face and neck. Some had rifles, but no one knew where the bullets were coming from until it was too late—their bodies buckled from the force of the shots, and they fell to the ground one after the other, piling up like bloody, hole-filled dominoes—shining rays of the sunrise cast on their mayhem and the burning embers of the jailhouse.

A couple of the men took cover and started shooting in Hungry and Dove's direction, so Hungry and Dove concentrated their fire until they shot all of their rivals in their heads. They looked at each other, smiling mischievously as their victim's hats flew sideways down the street. A couple of the guys who took shots in the belly lay squirming in the street as Hungry and White Dove closed in on the rest of them, laughing and shooting.

As they ran toward their targets, they circled the saloon and picked up all the stragglers. Most people were running for cover or heading home. A few of the gamblers and hookers were still at the bar, as were the barmaids and the bartender. Hungry and White Dove went to the train station and climbed onto the roof. They silently perched over the town's center and watched as the last embers of the jailhouse burned. All that was left was an iron cage and a metal locker—the rest of it was now ashes and coal. They watched the sunrise as they laid quietly together.

Hungry covered White Dove with a blanket so no one would notice her. They stayed hidden for several minutes until the streets were clear, and then they made their way toward the hotel. They wondered if they had just killed everyone that was after them—it had happened so fast. There were most likely a few that had slinked off to try and regroup for retaliation later, but at this point, it would be a few hours at least before they would do anything. They would go to the hotel, get a room and their saddlebags, and then go to the madam's house, where Hungry had lived as a kid, to see if any of the girls who helped raise him were there.

The walk wasn't very long—they walked the boardwalk, past the mercantile store around the block to the train station's platform. It looked empty and quiet; there were only a few people waiting to leave, but plenty waiting for the train's arrival.

They went to the back steps of the brothel. They were freshly built with new wood; you could smell the pine oil. The door was cracked open, and you could hear the clamoring from the girls inside the place.

One of them opened the door—it was Ruby. He could not believe it. He was astonished. She still looked kind and pretty even though it had seemed like a decade since he had seen her. She instantly recognized him, and they hugged. She was one of his favorite girls who had usually looked after him. He remembered when he had turned 12 and had gone to live out of town for the first time—he had missed their comfort.

He asked if any other girls were still around there, and Ruby nodded her head but then shook it. She explained that only three of the six remained alive. One was inside, but she had been having convulsions, and so she was always close to her bed. Her name was Emma, and she was either Russian or Yugoslavian. She had a thick accent and was always strict with him, but she had fed him well.

She looked her age, and her red lipstick was too bright-colored for her face. She, too, smoked cigarettes through a long fancy tube. She smiled at them, and Hungry could tell that she recognized him. Her eyes made their way over White Dove's body, her ample curves showing through her dress. Emma was impressed with her style, and you could see the appreciation in her eyes.

The other girl, Ruby told him, was in San Francisco, whom he had known as Maja. She was always kind to him and brought him hot food, knives, and toy guns. He used to sleep under her bed sometimes in winter months when it was freezing cold outside.

I'm born of worms, I'm born of worms, I'm born of worms, I'm born of worms.

He remembered her grabbing him from under the walking boards, half-frozen and starved, bringing him inside to the warmth of a wood stove, giving him hamburger soup for his belly. He would never forget her warmth and comfort. Hopefully, she would come back alive, or he would visit San Francisco and see her sometime.

They drank Chinese tea and smoked tobacco leaves from a hookah pipe. There were red, exotic lampshades hanging from the room, with gas lighting, flickering, and burning wicks even when it was daylight outside. The front entry had a giant granite stairway leading up to the huge oak double doors of the building. There was an escape tunnel under a rug that Hungry used to spend a lot of time in hiding, spying, exploring, and sleeping.

Ruby told them how the town mayor had killed the last sheriff for adulterous affairs with his wife and how the cattle rancher's brought wealth to the town. Gold was still shipped by train in crates to unknown places. There was the faint, familiar scent of hamburger stew brewing from the kitchen. Emma was cooking on a silver and black train car coal stove, and there were several other gals whom Hungry had never met. They all took in Dove; they gave her makeup and garments, and they all seemed to get along with her like they had been friends their whole life.

Ruby was sitting on a high-back, red leather couch with tiger claw feet. Next to Jack, she looked young for her 60-something age. She had had a taste of the Crystal water when Jack had bottled some the first time he had found the cave over twenty years ago. There still was a natural, 4-foot-long vein of gold in it. As a teenager, Jack had found his way into the cave through a hole the size of a rabbit's hole since he could comfortably get into such a tight space. The first time he robbed a coach, he had hidden the gold in that cave and had made a door out of earth and stones that you would never guess led to a cave entrance.

Ruby was laughing but then quieted her tone and started telling Jack how there were still no dogs in town after he had killed them all in his youth, and any that came into town after, he didn't quit killing them until he left Lincoln. As they were talking, all the girls came to the front of the grand room—they had made White Dove look like a goddess by dressing her in only white lace and jewels.

They opened a bookshelf revealing decanters of different spirits from around the globe. There was Irish whiskey, Russian vodka, Mexican tequila, and the good old American whiskey. They had other additives, which kept them mixing up the concoctions for hours. They were all well-informed about Jack "Hungry" Hollow. They were all treated respectfully in this town because of the way he would quickly murder anyone who gave them grief. He always gave them gold and jewels.

He had been gone for a while because when the first big cattle drives came through, he had killed half the horsemen that came with them. When he left, it was a mess and a massacre. Remembering back; there were wanted posters of him hanging everywhere. He had a few dozen cattlemen chasing after him in town. When the train whistle blew to clear the station, he headed for the steam engine and crossed the track barely in time to evade the cattlemen. He hopped on the train and climbed to the roof.

He broke a window and jumped into the first buggy he came to. It was the weapons depot. There were crates of hardware everywhere—shotguns, sharp 50's, pistols, rifles (mostly all Winchesters of every caliber), and crates of bullets. The train stopped violently, with the brakes screeching along the tracks. Hungry loaded the shotguns and the rifles and headed to the station side window of the next car.

Men were looking out the window when he entered. They were caught by the 12-gage buckshot and were pretty much blown apart. The train car had stopped now, and men were entering from all sides. Hungry gathered the weapons from the dead and reloaded the shotguns. He set one down for a repeater and picked off the closest cowboys. Bullets were flying past him, and he kept firing and switching guns. He moved around the train car, firing out the windows and down the aisles. Bodies were dropping through the room like flies as Hungry made his way to the engine room.

The engineer was about to leave the train when Hungry caught up to him and made him get the train rolling. He worked his way through the entire train and shot everyone who was not running for their lives. A never-ending supply of loaded guns and ammunition seemed to lay at his feet with all the dead cowboys. He threw bodies off as the train moved out of the station. He was in a whirlwind of adrenaline and kept the train engineer running the train and shoveling coal in the engine.

The train was headed toward Sacramento that time, and it was the first time he got away with literally a wagon-load of gold and made the papers—and the wanted list. He was thinking about leaving town again soon, not wanting to bring any trouble to the girls.

They were sampling the tonics and smoking herbs and tobacco. One girl sang, and another played a stringed instrument. The light shade burned a red glow. They all marveled at the beautiful work Alita had done with the jewels in Jack's teeth—it made him look wicked, mean, and damn good-looking, as Emma had told him when they sat together on the sofa.

Gargoyles and demon faces, carved in the dark hardwood of the crown molding, hung suspended in smoke as statues of naked angels stood in the corners of the room. Hungry gave Ruby a bag of gold coins to share with the house. She was the one who was the most like him, and she knew he would not stay long.

They went to the kitchen and ate hamburger stew. All the girls spoke to White Dove separately. They all hugged her and gave her several small, wrapped gifts. Jack held Emma and Ruby in a group hug—they were the closest thing to a family he had ever known. The girls had never liked his mom or gotten along with her, so he didn't ask about her, and they didn't offer any news.

It was going to be daylight soon. They were sad to be leaving and promised to return sooner the next time. They went to the hotel's stables and checked the stallion. He was waiting and was freshly brushed and fed; his coat was shiny white. He seemed to smile at them when they approached.

The stable boy appeared. He wasn't really a boy—just slow in the head. He was the same age as Jack and knew about his past. He admired Hungry for killing his drunk, cheating wife and abusive father, who definitely had it coming. He looked at them and said he wouldn't tell anyone anything—he didn't see anything or anyone, and that was all he knew. He saddled the horse and filled up extra canteens with freshly pumped water. Hungry gave him a few 20-dollar gold coins and a 4-inch ivory-handled pocket knife, which the Case brothers had just made that year.

They nodded their heads, mounted the stallion, and headed out of town. The sky was dark and patchy, with shades of gray and black, etching soft white highlights along its eastern edge. It was almost sunrise. Dove looked at Hungry in a slightly different light. She always admired him for everything he had done with her and for her, but she hadn't realized he was a hero to so many. He had always told her his story about growing up in the streets but never of what he did when he came of age.

They were going to the cave along the trail. The train

whistle blew in the distance. As the sun topped the mountains, it warmed the side of their faces. As they traveled, Hungry ate jerked beef and replayed the visit with Ruby, Emma, and the rest of the girls. They had done fairly well for the house.

When Hungry was a young boy, the house was run by Ruby's abusive husband. He was wealthy and cruel. The girls would have to sneak Hungry in at night when it was cold, and they would have to hide food for him, or he would beat them if he found out they were disobeying his word. He was found dead, his body full of holes and burning on the boardwalk one dark night. Hungry remembered with a smile that Ruby had been mad at him for a couple of days after they found his burnt body.

Chapter 12

The Follower

As daylight broke, they both caught a brief glimpse of their follower. It had been waiting outside the town to catch their scent again and follow them. Their stay in town didn't last long, but it was quite memorable. It was a tiger or an extremely large mountain lion, they pondered. It had let them have a quick view of it, but it was gone in an instant.

Their trail led them to a stream shrouded by another giant dogwood. Its blossoms covered the grassy knoll as freshly dropped flowers swirled in the pools of stream water before floating away downstream. Giant mossy rocks lined the waterway, and it had lush vegetation for the stallion to graze on while they took a break from traveling.

There was a storm coming in from the west. They could see the thunderheads forming with thick black clouds on the horizon. It turned the skies a couple of shades darker in an instant as the temperature of the air dropped. Hungry and Dove moved close together and breathed in the damp, colder air. The valley flashed with light as lightning lit up the horizon seconds after thunder rumbled and crashed with deep baritone tones, and then rain started to fall. It smelled clean and fresh.

They gathered all their belongings, mounted the stallion, and rode off to the hills. The trail had quickly turned slippery and muddy, so they unmounted and ran alongside each other. The stallion followed, snickering and snorting every so often. It kept its pace right behind them steadily, as did their other follower.

After winding around the canyon hillside, they came to an open cave. They were drenched when they entered it. They quickly lit fires and made torches to check the back of the cave for predators. It was home to a couple of raccoons that ran past them out into the rain. They took off their wet clothes and hung them by the fire on the makeshift drying rack they made out of sticks stuck into cracks in the rock wall. They wrapped themselves in dry pelts from their saddlebags and stayed close to the fire. Hungry dried all his weapons in front of the fire, making sure the bullets would not get too wet.

It was the first rain in months. They looked at each other with wet hair and half-naked bodies while a coyote howled in the distance. It was getting dark outside the cave, the reflecting light shimmering off the ground, illuminating the trail and hillside beyond. Luckily, someone had left empty wooden chests and a couple of broken wagon wheels behind, which they burned. There was enough room for all of them to be warm and dry inside the rock cave.

Suddenly, they heard a rumbling growl from outside. Yellow eyes pierced through the smoke exiting the cave's entrance. A flash of lightning illuminated the predator. It was no longer a mystery—it was a giant mountain lion the size of a small horse. It leaped toward them and took White Dove by the neck, then it was gone in a flash.

Hungry stood in disbelief for a second before gathering his guns and ammo and running out from the cave. He was moving faster than he ever had, and his heart was beating through his chest. He could see the trail up the mountainside, fresh tracks ripping through wet ground. He immediately started following the giant cat, running through bushes and thickets of trees over rocks and fallen logs.

He chased the trail, barely catching a glimpse of the animal and White Dove's white, flowing garments. There were blood drops here and there on the ground—he knew she was in trouble. This was the first time his sanctity had been invaded. He was running at full speed through the densely populated hillside. Sticks were breaking off in his face and arms, but he kept on going full speed.

After crashing through timbers over rocks and ledges, he finally came to a spot where he had seen the lion crouched over White Dove. Her shawl was mostly red with blood, and she was trembling. Suddenly, the animal backed away, and Hungry unloaded his bullets into it—piercing through the flesh, the bullets ripped, firing the animal apart.

He ran closer, firing fast with both barrels of his 45-caliber single-action revolvers. He saw arrows pierced through its side; she must have slowed it down with her quiver of arrows. Her shoulder and neck were lacerated and bleeding. Luckily, it had grabbed her from the back, so her jugular vein was still intact. She was waving her arms and moaning as he came to her, emptying his bullets into the giant cat.

He blasted the animal a few more times out of anger, scooping up now-red White Dove as he carried her to a grassy knoll close by. He wrapped her wounds with what was left of her garment and prayed that she would stay alive. He could feel her heartbeat as he held her close. He realized he was crying for the first time in many, many years, and he repeatedly told her to keep breathing and stay alive. The meat on the back of her neck was being held together by her wrappings, and they were all blood-soaked.

Rain was making it slippery as he headed back down the hill with her toward the cave. It had happened so fast that he could not believe the cat had attacked them. Her wounds were wrapped tightly with the makeshift bandages, but he knew something more was needed. Her eyes were glossy, looking up at him in fear and pain. She moaned and trembled in shock as they finally got to the mouth of the cave.

The white stallion was snorting and stomping his feet. Jack knew they had to go somewhere and find medicine as soon as possible. He gathered the supplies that they needed and hid the rest in the back of the cave under some rocks and boulders. He moved with an unhuman speed, carrying her as if she weighed nothing. He knew he had medical supplies at the Crystal Cave, and his chances were better going there instead of any town, where he would have to be on alert for a gunfight at any time. He mounted the stallion after wrapping her to his chest and arms, carrying her like a mother with an overgrown child. The horses knew where to go and wasted no time cutting a trail toward Auburn. Should he risk going into town? He knew she had lost too much blood and hoped that she would stay conscious. The white stallion broke into a smooth and steady gallop heading north.

The rain lightened, and the full moon illuminated the trail and white clouds in the distance. They pressed on at full speed. As the white stallion galloped smoothly ahead, Hungry thought of the medicine man he knew as a teenager and wondered if he was still in the town.

After a few hours of travel, they reached the Indian village that was close to the town of Auburn. Hungry readied his pistols in case of any other enemy encounters. Pressing far past the caves of the troglodytes and on into the friendly encampment of the Maidu Indians, he rode into the village as warriors watched him with curiosity, knowing that he was in dire trouble and posed no threat as his front was completely red with blood. White Dove's long hair was flowing in the air, partially matted with dried blood.

He stopped next to a warrior to ask for the chieftain. He said "medicine man" over and over as they looked at him in disbelief. One of the warriors came forward to him and pointed to a teepee in the distance. The Shaman came forward from it and motioned them inside.

The firelight reflected off the animal skin walls, and the warmth immediately surrounded them. They were both shivering from the cold and from shock. Hungry unraveled the ties that held White Dove to him, and, holding her in his arms, he looked at the medicine man and asked for help—it was indeed the same healer he had known as a boy, the one who had always been kind to him.

Females entered the cave with water and fresh linen, and they laid White Dove on a makeshift cot of animal pelts and tree leaves. They attended to her deepest wounds first: teeth marks piercing her cheek and the bleeding lacerations on the back of her neck. They cleaned her wounds and re-wrapped them, adding policies and sacred medicines to keep her from bleeding anymore and getting an infection. She was still moaning, and her body was limp; she had lost too much blood. Hungry believed in the medicine man's magical powers and hoped with all of his soul that she would not perish.

The girls added wood to the fire and began chanting in rhythm. All of them had known of White Dove long before the half-faced man with jagged teeth brought her in. They had a silent respect for them as they were outsiders, different from all of the other Indians and whites whom they had come across. They knew White Dove was the daughter of an Iroquois whose mother was born of the Troglodytes and had escaped their wrath and the hell of living underground to wander the above grounds alone. They also knew that she was a fierce warrior and had fought many battles just to stay alive, so they would fight this battle to try to keep her daughter alive.

They looked at Hungry, the jewels in his teeth reflecting the glow of the fire. He had lacerations on his face and arms from running through the brush. They tended to him, pulling out the slivers and chunks of wood and applying the medication of herbs and roots. Their faces were painted with war paint, and Hungry's with blood and polis as all of their eyes were reflecting the glow of firelight.

He openly grimaced, trying to share her pain and give her relief. He still had the dented metal canteen with Crystal water and whiskey in his saddle bag. He retrieved it and had her sip slowly from it as he did, too. Instantly, her eyes opened wider and seemed more alive. Her heartbeat elevated, and she stopped shaking.

He knew the crystal cave spring water was something truly magical—even the Shaman looked at him and the canteen in awe. It smelled of whiskey, which was not a favorite of the Indians, but they all had seen that it had helped her immensely and sat quietly, staring in disbelief. She looked at them and whispered "thank you" in their dialect as she stared at the exiting smoke going up through the hole of the teepee. The air of the small room smelled of fresh herbs, polis, and eucalyptus woodsmoke.

Warriors gathered the white stallion and corralled it with the rest of their horses. He didn't seem to mind the company. Hungry thought about the cabin hidden in the rocky nest on the mountaintop and knew they had to get there.

After they had rested for a few hours, they smoked from a ceremonial pipe and drank mixtures of roots and medicines. The smoke exiting the room swirled and twisted as it rose. The air was thick with the smell of burning sage and other medical herbs. The firelight cast shadows on the side walls of the teepee of giant bucks, grizzly bears, and wolves.

The wind howled outside, shaking the canvas of wildlife, making them seem more alive. The ground started shaking, and Hungry snapped back to the present as he recognized the sound of hooved animals running toward them. He quickly gathered his guns and ammunition, winked at White Dove, and slipped through the door in a flash.

He saw horsemen with painted faces carrying spears and tomahawks. They were not from the Maidu Tribe; they were an enemy band of warriors, raiding camps to steal the women, guns, gold, and liquor. They were so close that the smell of their horses was overpowering. They smelled of rotting flesh and death.

Instantly, Hungry started shooting the fast-approaching riders in their heads, small holes in the pierced flesh, blowing huge pieces out of the back of their heads. Blood, skull bones, and brains splattered behind the riders, making them slide off their horses sideways to be shot in the same fashion.

Tomahawks flew from the tribe warriors who had joined the battle. There were men and women shooting arrows and throwing tomahawks. The men on horseback were getting thin—a few tried lighting torches to burn teepees and corrals, but the warriors of the Maidu Tribe were slaughtering the intruders.

Hungry killed the first dozen riders, blasting their heads apart with his 44 cal. Hollow-point bullets he had made himself. The men and women of the tribe looked at him in fear and admiration. Hungry smiled the wickedest grin at them through his jagged smile of diamonds, ruby, and electro.

Once the fighting was over, he went back into the teepee and stayed close to White Dove as she smiled and closed her eyes to sleep. The chief came to honor Hungry with baskets of dried rabbit and dear meat. He knew how much Hungry liked dried meats. The chief was as old as the mountains. He was tall and skinny, with buckskin paints and beaver skin moccasins, eagle feathers weaved in his headdress hung across his leathery reddish-brown skin. His eyes were like those of a hawk, piercing into your soul, wise and all-knowing. He always seemed nice to Hungry, so he gave him some pistols and ammo from his saddlebags and said, "Friends always." The warriors celebrated their quick victory, and all the dead were carted off to be left to the wolves.

The medicine man told Hungry he would watch over Dove until his return or until she healed enough to travel. Hungry wanted to check the caves and the hidden cabin in the mountains. He would check the Crystal Cave and get more water for them, he thought, and then go to check the cabin before returning to Dove. He hoped that her deep wounds would be completely healed soon.

He rolled smokes and handed a few out as he surveyed the trail in his mind. It wasn't far—over the canyon from where he was now to the great American rivers—and would probably take him a day of riding. It was a good plan. He went back into the teepee to say his goodbyes. The Shaman was his oldest friend, and Hungry knew he could trust him with White Dove. He collected his gear and all the gifts he could fit in his saddle bags and made his way toward the river and the Crystal Cave.

The stallion took to the trails at a fast gallop. The previous night's rain had made the ground soft, leaving an earthy, musk scent in their nostrils. They headed east under gunmetal gray skies, with fading clouds on the horizon. Hungry had quite the exciting day and knew he could stand a few hours of traveling before sunrise.

As soon as the trail started winding through the canyons, they slowed to try and start looking for a dry place to camp. The air grew colder the closer they got to the river. The great America's two forks joined only a few hundred yards away from one of his other favorite caves. He had its entrance covered with giant slabs of boulders that required horses to be moved. It would be on his list of entrances to check on in the morning.

They found a spot under the overhanging ledge with a giant boulder blocking the wind, and they ate their gifts of food. Hungry gave the white stallion the sweet cornbread from his food bag provided by the Maidu Tribe women. He thought of White Dove as he drifted off to sleep.

Chapter 13

The Under Dwellers

The night was eerie quiet. White Dove lay in her wrappings of animal pelts and furs. She was awakened by something, but now there was only quiet. No one else was in the teepee. She slowly opened her eyes and looked at the burnt embers of coals in the fire pit. The fire had gone out, and a faint tendril of white smoke rose in the air. Suddenly, she heard gunshots, then horses' hooves beating the ground. She struggled to get up, but it was painful; the lacerations from the mountain lion were healing fast, but they were still stinging and painful.

She managed to get up and get a better view of the inside walls of the rawhide. Animal skins, herbs, and grindstones aligned the room. White Dove saw her quiver of arrows for her bow and arrows as well as her perfume bottle igniter. She lifted her arms gently, wincing in pain as she did so. Whimpering, she realized she had to get through it; horse hooves were growing closer, so she scooted as far back from the opening as she could. Grabbing her bow and arrows along the way, she placed all of the furs and pelts around her body for support, gathered more weapons, and placed them at her side just as the opening of the teepee revealed two crazy-eyed cattlemen. They had a large knife in one hand and a pistol in the other. They forced an Indian girl into the teepee and were smiling and laughing wickedly. They looked back when suddenly their skulls were ripped apart by tomahawks, making the horrifying sound of rock crunching bone. At the same time, White Dove let out arrows that flew into their necks and chests.

Blood streaked down the cattlemen's faces from the tomahawks wedged in the skulls, and arrows stuck out from their necks and faces. White Dove felt initially relieved until she noticed the tomahawk users. They were screaming in a strangled, high-pitched screech, with bones jutting jaggedly from scarred face tissue. Their skin was pale and riddled with mutilations: eyelids removed, facial bones sunken in, and piercings of bones and shells growing into the skin. Their eyes were milky white and glossed over as they came through the doorway, their arms outstretched like zombies.

The cattlemen's bodies were being dismembered and wrapped in cowhide torn off the walls of the teepee. Other Under-dwellers with torches set ablaze the place, wearing necklaces made of body parts. They had their faces painted with the blood and carnage of their latest victims. They were the Under-dwellers from the Osenca clan of troglodytes, who were the craziest and most deadly of all known cannibals. They had come to raid the camp. Apparently, they had been watching and waiting to strike at the same time the cattlemen made their move; they followed in and now left the whole camp in a disarray of death and massacre.

Somehow, White Dove had slept through the sound of the first intruders in her fever and delirium. She was trying to reload an arrow when she was quickly grabbed up and wrapped in cowhide, her arms wrapped tightly beside her body, her face bagged and wrapped though she could see a little through one eye out of a small hole. Her mouth made a muffled sound, but something round in a thin-skinned pouch was stuffed into it. She could barely breathe around it or through her nose. There was no chance to get loose or fight back, and everything was starting to go dark as she could feel herself being scooped up. The pain shot through her body, burning until she completely fainted and was loaded into a wagon with the rest of the wrapped bodies. She came to, seeing a couple of them were other smaller women, one with a child, and there were pieces of warriors' and cattlemen's arms, legs, chests, and heads wrapped like meat from a butcher in animal skins.

In her horror, White Dove realized they were in the chuckwagon. They were meat for this crazed band of under-dwelling flesh eaters. White Dove came to consciousness again. She could feel the wagon moving fast. Whenever it hit bumps, the arrows wrapped inside her hides cut into the skin on the side of her face; her arms were still wrapped too tight to move. All she could do was try to breathe. The wagon began to move faster, and she faded to black again. The ride got really bumpy and painful before it stopped. She faded in and out of consciousness several times as the side of her face became pretty cut up from the arrowhead.

She came to consciousness again, this time to the sound of tribal drums, chanting, and high shrill screams. There was also a constant clanking of metal on rock. White Dove was naked, being forced to drink from a green-colored gourd; the concoction tasted earthy and grainy, slightly bitter. She was being treated for her wounds with a marriage of mud and ground roots and berries. She could smell a slight sweetness to the potion they applied to her. She was in a cavern who knew how far underground. There were no candles or light whatsoever, just a tiny amount of illumination bouncing down the cavern walls from the torchlights and fire at the beginning of the cave. Hands were rubbing across her face and body, and before she realized she was wrapped in animal hide again.

A loose fragment of an arrow with the arrowhead attached was embedded into the cowhide, and she had enough room to wiggle to grab it in her hand. She moved it to her armpit and clenched her arm down on it hard just as they tightened her wraps. She was placed in a small opening in the front part of the cave. After a while, she could hear the moaning of the other captives—they were being tortured and butchered; some were being carved up and eaten raw. She listened to the drone of the drum beat and the clang of metal, the shrilling and chanting, every once in a while hearing a scream or moan from a captive. She was bound at the ankles, and her mouth was still gagged. She was bandaged well, still in one piece, and miraculously, her wounds were not bleeding, although they still hurt terribly and had a burning itch.

Outside the cave, the full moon was white against the backdrop of the dark, cobalt sky. There were few stars in the night—a couple, the really bright ones, shined green and red. Gray, billowy clouds outlined the skyline. Torches blazed in the gnarled and bloodstained hands of many of the Under Dwellers, their tattooed and pierced crimson faces shrieking in madness while feasting on the raw flesh of the cattlemen and other captives.

There, over towering cliffs, the high priestess watched through the opening of the passage, seeing through the flickering of red and orange flames to the dwindling pile of mutilated bodies dumped from the chuck wagon down below. It was now on its side and was ablaze. Huge burning logs in a circle of rocks and giant clay pots of blood and intestines, organs also burned brightly. Some of their flames were turning green and yellow at the tips as they rose towards the night sky. The priestess watched from above but did not take part in the ceremony. She ate a piece of partially chard rib meat from one of the captives. She was sipping from a skull cup of red liquid and curiously preoccupied with her new captive. She sensed a familiarity in this one, and if she was going to be consumed, she would have to be free of infections.

Hungry reached the American riverbank by early morning. After a quick couple of hours of shut-eye in the rock shelter, he ate more dried meat and walked with the white stallion for a mile. He kept feeling an unexplainable sense of urgency, so after walking a short while, he climbed back on the white stallion and made quick tracks to the first cave.

The caverns entrance was hard to find—almost completely hidden since the natural grass and brush had grown over the opening. He knew it was sealed well, so he kept traveling to the next one. He traveled along the riverside for hours and checked the cave opening with the Gatling gun—it was still sealed up tight even though they had left in a hurry. He had done a good job placing boulders and fresh-rooted shrubs in the right places to promote growth; it looked natural.

After another short ride, he came to the area of the Crystal Cave. There was another cave fairly close that he rode to. He unsaddled the stallion and made a little dry camp before heading off to check the Crystal Cave. On his walk, he thought of White Dove, wishing he knew if she was up and moving yet. It had only been a few days since her attack, but their wounds healed stupid fast, and he knew the crystal water had something to do with it. He was going to bring a couple of canteens of the pure water back—one for his Indian shaman friend and one for White Dove. He was going to drink a few shots of it when he got there, too, he thought to himself.

He checked his guns and covered his tracks as he got closer to the cave entrance. It, too, was just how they left it—fortunately undisturbed. A couple of small animal holes made it easy for him to peel back the rocks and brush, making sure to set them aside gently so he could replace them. The rain had loosened up the soil, and he was inside quickly. He lit a lantern and walked it through the passageways, working himself into the farther recesses of the cavern. It was lonelier without his White Dove, he realized. He didn't stop to look at any of his treasures; he just made his way back to the Crystals.

Hungry could smell a sulfur, pungent, earthy smell, and could see a faint light emanating from the crystals. They were giant and colorful. The stream of water was as it always was: slightly steaming, twisting, and swirling through tiny passageways of the crystals. It started from the cave's back wall and poured into a smaller pool, where he collected it inside a canteen. After a few minutes, he filled the second canteen, drank a good part of it, and then refilled it.

His head swirled a little bit, and all of the events of the past few days played through his mind in a fast sequence. He knew he had better get back to White Dove, so he did not take extra time after filling the canteen. He worked his way to the front of the cave. It was a good 20 minutes at a fast pace, and he knew the passage as well, so he made a pact to come back with White Dove and spend some time—maybe change his boots in for some other exotics since these ones were getting a little worn.

He patched up the entrance of the cave and added some extra bushes to the front to hide the freshly placed soil and rocks. Then, after covering his tracks well, he headed back to the white stallion. The stallion was snickering and stomping his feet. Hungry was also uneasy about something, so he pulled out his six guns and headed to high ground. He climbed up the ridge of the mountainside quietly and scouted. There were no signs of anyone, so he laid down on a rock outcropping on the hillside and remained perfectly still for about half an hour. There was still no movement or sound, so he started slowly going back down to the cave.

The white stallion looked at him, snorted, and stomped one hoof. Hungry hurriedly picked up camp. After checking to see if all his guns were loaded and scouting a little bit in every direction until he was satisfied nobody was around or spying on him, he mounted the stallion and started heading west to leave the river canyon. Once again, he had this ominous feeling that he needed to get back to White Dove as soon as possible. He quickened his horse's stride on the path.

The sun was high in the sky, and its warmth made mist rise from Valley as they steadily rode on the trail. After leaving the winding canyon trails behind them, they broke into a fast gallop, heading back down the foothills of the Sierra mountain range.

They stopped to drink water at a ravine just outside of Auburn. A little bit down the ravine, there was a campsite with a canvas tent and a couple of horses. There were a couple of dirty cowboys, with a skinny girl that looked scared and homely. Hungry walked the stallion up to their camp, and the taller cowboy told him to beat it and that they didn't take kindly to drifters or anyone else poking their noses in their business.

Hungry turned his head and flashed them a smile through his jagged, ripped skin and grill of jewels. The fatter cowboy held the girl by the wrist and was telling her to be quiet and go into the tent. Hungry drew out and pointed his 45-caliber pistols right at each of their heads. He said, "Now, suppose that the girl does not wanna go into the tent—maybe she doesn't want to be with you gentlemen at all. Let's hear her opinion on that."

She immediately looked at Hungry, crying, and said, "No, I do not want to be with these heathens; they killed my parents and have kept me as their captive for over two weeks now."

The fat one was reaching for his gun, but Hungry immediately put a bullet right through the center of his forehead. He also shot him in the heart while his other hand ripped lead through the taller cowboy's face and neck. They died pretty quickly; in fact, they never touched their pistols or had a chance to raise a rifle. Their bodies were both bleeding from the headshots and twitching in the dirt. The skinny one seemed to bleed a lot more.

Hungry asked the girl if she knew her way back to town. He took a couple of Winchester rifles from their saddlebags and kept the fat man's six guns and gun belt. They were colts and held large bullets just the way he liked. They had good horses, too. The girl said she had family in Auburn, so he left her with two loaded pistols and dragged off the bodies of the dead. He stripped most of the clothes off them and left them in an opening where buzzards and coyotes would get to them.

Soon, he returned to the camp, and the girl said she could ride a horse well, so he helped her into the saddle of the healthiest-looking one. He took a few extra minutes, showed her how to use the pistols, and gave her a shotgun lesson. He told her he had a pressing issue and could not escort her to town, but she would be safe as long as she hurried along the trail and "shot first and asked questions later" if any shifty-looking characters approached her.

She looked at him peculiarly, but she knew she was in a much better place, so she thanked him for his generosity and prepared the saddlebags for the trail. He tipped his hat and headed back on the trail. He coaxed the white stallion into a gallop and headed west again.

After a few hours of speedy travel, they came to a stop, noticing fresh tracks at an intersection. Hungry could see where a wagon and several horses had cut across the trail in the dirt, going down into the canyon below. He stopped there for a while and looked at the tracks. They were odd—only a day or two old and looked as if they were made by someone driving wild or out of control, going as fast as they could, or a driver who was painfully inexperienced. They came from the direction he was traveling in but cut down the canyon and made their own trail over the dry brush and grassy hillsides through the Manzanita Scrub oaks.

He looked back at the dirt. There appeared to be blood drops every so often—something was bleeding. He quickened his pace along the trail back to the Maidu encampment. His heart was racing as fast as the hooves of his white stallion. Galloping like the wind, they flew across hillsides and through valleys and ravines. When he arrived at the encampment, he could tell straightaway that things were not right.

Several Indian warriors from the Maidu tribe were standing guard before the village. Hungry spoke to them, and they told him about how they were raided, first by the cattlemen gang and then by the cave dwellers, and how the latter had taken White Dove, along with other men, females, and children. They had massacred a lot of their warriors, but the Maidu tribe was planning their retaliation, waiting for the next full moon and for some of their warriors to heal. They would attack them the next came out of their caves, the warriors explained.

Hungry couldn't wait that long. He asked if the shaman had survived. They replied that they could not find him and that he would be one of the first they would have eaten for his knowledge. Hungry shook his head, made gestures of peace, and headed back quickly to where he had seen the tracks. There were still a couple of hours of daylight, and he needed to use them to find the Under Dweller's village.

Chapter 14

Preparing The Feast

The Under Dwellers continued their ceremonial macabre throughout the twilight and into the night as the fires burned coals to ashes. They roasted different parts of their human collection on giant metal spears, bamboo poles, and metal disks that held arms, organs, and legs. Other blood-stained, smoking wooden racks held ribs and backbones. It was a grotesque display of human carnage, covered in spices and herbs, milky white eyes shining upward. The older female Under Dweller would collect the cooked meat on giant metal and wooden pans and debone it, forming huge piles of bones that they all sucked on and threw into the fire.

The smell of burning bones and flesh filled the cave air. The queen and her servant kept White Dove alive. They moved her closer to the opening of the cave, where the smell grew stronger. She could now see the reflected firelight dancing on the damp cavern walls. It slowly illuminated the darkness, and she could see other captives wrapped in animal hides, with only small portions of their heads and eyes showing, pupils glowing with fear, faces pale with horror.

All of the body parts were being cooked or eaten raw while their hosts were being kept alive. Only two captives besides herself were visibly all in one piece. The creatures wanted them to see the horror that awaited them; the three were all in a hallucinogenic state, intoxicated from the drink they were being forced to consume.

The fires, red and orange colors, were super bright. Once her eyes finally adjusted to the light, the sound came in waves, louder and then soft. Her eyes were taking in the horror show as she watched the cannibals feasting on her friends and enemies while slithering entwined with each other in a seemingly sensual orgy. She really needed a smoke right now, she thought to herself as she screamed into her gag.

Hungry stopped at the wagon tracks. He realized his hands were shaking once again; he had a sense of déjà vu, thinking back to when he was chasing the jaguar. He was scared he would not find her alive. He followed the tracks down the hillside and into a darkening valley. For hours, he rode horseback in the dark until he realized he had to be within a mile of the place. There were broken pieces of the carriage here and there on the rocks, and the blood trail was getting thicker. He could see well enough even with the sky being clouded by the dark, thick smoke. He stopped by some boulders and took a drink from the canteen. He could see the smoke rising from their fires far in the distance.

He crept closer as the full moon revealed itself from

behind rock-faced canyon walls. Their cave system was dug into the cliffs on the mountainside. They were all spread out in a line and built up on top of one another, like a crude, honeycomb structure, but with only a few visible openings. They were all formed around a bigger center cave, where the fires were burning brightest. Hungry walked toward the fires. He was carrying a lot of weight in lead and iron. As he got closer, he could hear their shrill howls and screams and he could smell the scent of cooked flesh. He hoped like hell it wasn't his White Dove.

Hungry had to make a good plan this time; there was no room for error. If she was still alive, he had to get there quickly. He set his eyes on the center cave, the one with the big opening. He could see figures moving inside of it every once in a while, but he noticed that most of the patrons of this cannibal circus freak show were outside. He wondered if he had enough bullets for everyone. As he approached in silence, he took out his knives and tomahawks; he was going to make his first kills as silently as possible in order to not bring attention to himself.

He walked closer to the cave system. He had been on the exact opposite side of the time before when he had spied on their encampment, so he knew the layout pretty well. He followed a tree line to an opening where several troglodytes were sensually entwined in each other's arms. He quickly threw the tomahawks at each one, aiming at their necks. He then rushed in with his knives and quickly hushed the remaining two with quick thrusts to their hearts.

He collected his tomahawks from the bodies and faded into the shadows. He counted again and prepared to approach the next group. They were too preoccupied with their sickening fetishes to defend themselves from the onslaught of Hungry's mayhem. He continued on his course, slashing with tomahawks and straight razors until one of the Under Dwellers finally let out a wicked high-pitched shrill that must have been an intruder alert.

They seemed to snap out of their trance collectively and started focusing their energy on finding an intruder. Hungry kept on slashing throats and piercing hearts as he moved mechanically through the crowds. He blended into the shadows, disguised himself with their blood, and used a shield he had found on one of the bodies. He worked his way like a sickle cutting through the wheat, moving close to the opening of the center cave.

He finally started using his guns carefully, not wasting any bullets. He shot them each one time right in the sweet spot: in the dead center of their eyes. Some went crossed-eyed, some had their eyes rolling back into their heads, some spread straight or sideways. Their twisted, dark lights were being extinguished.

He continually fired until his fingers and hand grew

sore, and he was almost out of bullets. He noticed the pile of bones from bodies eaten that had been tossed into the fire and continued to kill every last one of them he could find. He found a torch and looked into the main entrance of the cave. Hungry could see a couple of wrapped bodies looking back at him through the light.

He watched another troglodyte taking her own life. Her mutilated body reflected her twisted image in a broken glass mirror as she disemboweled herself over a platter. Hungry looked around and reloaded his pistols. He took off a few of the empty bullet Bandoleros in order to lighten his load. He stuck to only four pistols and loaded them with all of the bullets he had left.

White Dove's muffled voice gave him chills. He started unwrapping her once he recognized her blue and grey eyes. All colors seemed to mesh into one in the firelight, but he knew they were hers the second he'd seen them. She was alive! He checked her wounds and kissed her body and some of her cuts and bruises. She trembled—she was still feeling a little dizzy from the drug they had given her, but she was smiling and crying with happiness upon seeing Hungry. He rolled and lit a cigarette for her, and she looked at him and said, "We burn this place." A last single tear rolled down her cheek, revealing a pale streak where it removed her dried blood.

He unwrapped the other girl who was from the village. She was also trembling and crying. Hungry looked for any more cave dwellers. He shot any of them that were moving and looked around at all of the carnage. This place was pure evil, he thought. He had to end their kind. He gave White Dove a canteen of crystal water and told her to drink. She did as he told her. Her quivering arms could barely hold it due to shock and dehydration, but she could actually stand on her own after a few minutes. The other Maidu girl was given a drink of the crystal water, and she became more calm.

They had been so close to dying that having been saved was a surreal feeling. Hungry looked at all the bodies; it was too much work to pile them up and burn or bury them. He could not wait to leave this place and let the animals and time clean it up. He spread melted tallow, found in a clay pot underneath the roasting bodies, over all of the dead Under Dwellers at the entrance of the cave, and gathered anything else that looked like it would burn. He piled it all in the back of the big cave and lit it on fire with a torch. He would never come back here, he thought to himself. He picked up White Dove, climbed down the ledge from the cave, and then helped the Indian girl. They took one last look around as Hungry bent over and picked up White Dove, kissed her on the lips, and then started carrying her to the meadow. She gripped his arms and looked into his emerald green eyes.

He walked across the mutilated bodies of the Under Dwellers, making his way to the meadow where he had left the white stallion. The Indian girl followed, gathering weapons from the dead. Hungry was sure that he had killed every one of them he encountered, but he still felt uneasy and hastened to get out of there. There were others hidden underground, most likely their youngest and oldest. They would have plenty to eat for the next few months.

Hungry thought about the trapper cabin hidden in the canyon on the mountainside and wondered if it was still secure. They would go there soon after returning to the Maidu Village. He would share his crystal water with the shaman if he was there. He was hoping the shaman was still alive.

They took it slow, walking the white stallion two at a time on its back. They ate dried meat and bread and drank from the canteen of the Crystal water. White Dove's wounds were healing astonishingly fast. She said that they felt tight and itchy, but they were not as painful and were not infected. They looked weeks old already. She stretched her arms and neck as long as she could while riding the white stallion. Hungry admired her sleek, ample figure. He rolled and lit another smoke and handed it to her.

They all talked to one another as they traveled. The Indian girl's name was Tala—she was also called "grey wolf." She explained how her father had trapped a wolf cub on the day of her birth, and she told them how she had raised it for many moons until its years ran out and it grew too old to move its legs and perished. It was a sad tale of how all animals were on a different time clock. Even humans—our bodies cannot help but finally succumb to the relentless, grasping arms of Father Time. Some of us age much faster than others. We must always grab hold of each moment and precious memory, savor and enjoy it, and make it count.

A large, reddish-brown stray dog crossed their path, and Hungry rubbed his face subconsciously, feeling his jeweled teeth through the scarred hole in his face. For the first time, he felt empathy for a dog. He didn't have the urge to shoot it; he was just going to watch it pass and hope it found food or its owner.

Chapter 15

Salt And Sand

The years passed on fast, like tiny grains of sand falling through an hourglass, trickling down one by one, faster and faster. The trapper cabin was just how they had left it, other than the cobwebs and dust and other tiny furry creatures that had moved in. The spring brought lush green vegetation, colorful wildflowers, and plenty of animals to hunt and eat. They had stayed a couple of days at the camp by the ravine on the way back from returning Tala to her village.

The canvas tent, fire ring, and cooking equipment were still there. The girl and the horses were gone, buzzards circled in the distance, the dog was still there, standing at the crossroads. He now smiled at them from the porch of the cabin, revealing his long white canines. Several years had passed, and he looked a little older and had some grey in his fur. The dog had followed them quietly through the rock crevices up and up the rocky cliff embankments to their hidden retreat; he was part of their tribe now.

The trapper cabin was warm and comfortable. It looked like one of the famous oil paintings Hungry had in his cavern hideout. Hungry had used large cobblestones to build a hearth, covering the outside walls five feet up.

The cabin had huge milled wooden doors and a giant oak mantle. There was the fresh smell of roasted rabbit and quail. White Dove was preparing salad greens. She had not aged a bit, and her wounds had completely healed; her eyelid had even miraculously grown back long eyelashes. She spent a lot of her time hunting and making arrows, gardening, cooking, practicing herbalism and medicine, and, of course, collecting herbs. She had ferns growing on the outside of the cabin and a whole array of garden vegetables.

Some animals, including owls, hummingbirds, ground squirrels, and chickens, stayed around the cabins. Hungry never really liked squirrel meat, so they were the lucky ones. Hungry had not seemed to age either. He was still as sharp in mind and fast as lightning with his pistols. He was always busy with his routine and still ate an insatiable amount of meat – hardly any vegetables. They kept a canteen of the crystal water and took drinks from it now and again. It always made the hair on their neck stand and gave them goose pimples.

White Dove and Hungry would look at each other with bright glowing eyes and smile completely. In the evening, they would watch the light play on the ceiling, dancing from the electric firewire through the Mason jars he had brought. He had a lot of his favorite things from the caves to marvel at, including miniature steam engines he could tinker with; there were small mechanical animals that walked and flew, tiny boxes that made electricity with magnetic perpetual motion. Some captured energy from the sun and converted it to electricity. He had brought some of the clothes and jewelry from the crystal cave and incorporated some of the newest turn-of-the-century inventions into their home, such as one of the very first washing machines for soiled laundry. Hungry had already piped water from an uphill spring through his cabin, and some of it went through the woodstove and heated whenever the fire burned. Several boxes of animal skins and furs stacked against one wall were always drying on the mantle and outside walls. Hungry had them separated and cleaned before storing them in wooden boxes.

He exchanged these items for supplies at the local mercantile stores, making trips into town every few weeks to restock and inspect the trails leading to the entrances of his hidden caves. Hungry had downsized a few of the hideouts, moving his gold closer to the cabin and burying it by huge boulders on the mountain with animal shapes to help him remember where they were. He had so much hidden loot he could afford anything they wanted. It seemed all the people chasing him had grown old and died or moved away, or he had killed them. He was still always looking over his shoulder and disguising his appearance, always practicing with his guns daily. A huge assortment of them hung on the cabin walls above the fireplace over his whiskey still.

The cabin had lead glass windows placed in the perfect spot to let in the morning sun. Crystals on the windowsill would reflect prisms of rainbows. The white stallion was still looking strong and healthy for its old age. Hungry did not ride him very much, though, as they had a couple of smaller horses they would ride that could fit easier through the canyons' rock crevices.

Hungry would go to the meadow below the mountain to hunt for rabbits; they were getting scarce around the cabin. He would wrangle up a dozen or more to eat once a week and trade their skins for root beer, tobacco, sugar, yeast, corn candy, and beer. He would always conceal his face, which had actually grown back a little of his cheek and lip. Before, he had used a skin patch White Dove had made for him to hide his jeweled grimace. Nowadays, he had to open his lips for one to see it. There was a historical occasion many years before when Hungry had the opportunity to clear his name from the wanted ads and put an end to the endless bounty hunters, army Rangers, and lawmen he had to slay.

Hungry set up a Wells Fargo stagecoach complete with a driver and box of gold, then he drove it into town disguised as the bank coachman. When he got close to the sheriff's station, he screamed he was being robbed. He fired some shots from his shotgun and headed into the alleyway. He had acquired the carriage a few years back, stolen most of the gold, and hid it out, covered with lots of tree limbs; he was surprised years later to find it with a box of gold still in it. White Dove and he had come up with that plan while drinking his whiskey-infused root beer and smoking tobacco.

The year was 1893 when the town folks thought they had Hungry Jack Hollow trapped inside that cargo carriage and burned it to the ground with kerosene and alcohol. It was a well-played ruse, acted out by one of his oldest friends and a local call girl from the town. She had yelled out, "That is Jack Hollow in that carriage, robbing it for the gold!" A few local townsmen and the new sheriff were quick to surround it and fill it full of lead, shooting it many times. After it was filled with holes, they set it on fire and hooped and hollered. One of the town men died in the crossfire of bullets, and a few were wounded, but no one seemed to pay them any attention. They stood there watching the blaze, hooting and hollering.

One could see many shiny gold bars appear as the wooden boxes disintegrated into ash and coal. The smell of charred wood and burning flesh filled the air. Digging through the charred embers and bones after the incineration, the town's sheriff raised the skull of a smoldering skeleton, proclaiming, "These are the bones of Hungry Jack Hollow. He will no longer be a menace to this town or any other." Small jewels of diamond and ruby fell from the charcoal teeth of the smoking skull. The townspeople gathered and gossiped; some of them excited, some of them relieved, some of them saddened, and some of them just learning the story of the legend of Jack Hollow.